UNNATURAL RESOURCES

UNNATURAL RESOURCES

MINDY UHRLAUB

THE PERMANENT PRESS
Sag Harbor, NY 11963

For information, address:
 The Permanent Press
 4170 Noyac Road
 Sag Harbor, NY 11963
 www.thepermanentpress.com

Library of Congress Cataloging-in-Publication Data

 Uhrlaub, Mindy, author.
  Unnatural resources / Mindy Uhrlaub.
  Sag Harbor, NY: The Permanent Press, [2020]
   Includes bibliographical references.
  ISBN: 9781579626402 (cloth)
  ISBN: 9781579626426 (ebook)

 PS3621.H75 U56 2020 (print)   2020031912
 PS3621.H75 (ebook)   2020031913
 DDC 813'.6—dc23

Printed in the United States of America

This book is dedicated to my Nanee, Sharon Weinberg,
who taught me about gritty determination and
gave me the gift of languages.

A NOTE TO READERS

For generations, colonists from around the world have taken advantage of unrest in Africa. Violent militia takeovers of villages allow foreign entities to pillage natural resources. The result is rape, slavery, poverty, illness. Many African countries do not have an organized military to fight subjugation of locals. While this book is a work of fiction, it speaks to the brutality with which we treat each other. Although in Congo in this fictionalized story, The City and The Army could be in many places in the world.

TABLE OF CONTENTS

PART ONE

Therese

CHAPTER ONE

〰〰〰

"Where is Virgil? He was supposed to help me in the market today," Justine asked Mama. She struggled to lift the banana basket to her head. Her knees knocked, and her thighs quivered under the weight. The most recent of her stillbirths at home had drained Justine of her usual energy. Mama positioned Justine's basket over her tall, reedy friend's head and helped her to her feet.

"He's with Therese and Felix in the field." Mama never had any trouble hoisting her own cassava basket. She was short and strong with powerful arms and broad shoulders. "We'll find him on the way to market."

Their flip-flops sent up dust behind them, but even on gravel, the women were sure-footed as they carried the loads on their heads. They stopped on the road and listened. It wasn't long before they heard laughter in the fields.

"No fair, Virgil! You cheated!" cried Felix.

"Well, how am I supposed to read this when it's in English?" Virgil argued. The sound of small feet approached the women. Therese burst through the woody shrubs. Her green dress, usually worn to church, was covered in dust. At eleven, she was a baby giraffe with long, slender legs and a short upper body. She clutched a piece of stationery in her hand.

"He's never going to get this game, Mama!" Therese complained. As much as she loved the boys, playing with them could be annoying. They always ganged up on her. Mama held out her arms for a hug.

"You're older than he is. Be patient." Mama rubbed her daughter's narrow back. Plumes of dust rose from Therese's dress. Mama knew that soon Therese would be a woman, but until then, she could play like the child she was. Still, she warned, "Therese, you shouldn't wear your Sunday dress into the field. Please wash it before supper."

"Virgil!" Justine called. The cassava field was still. She rested her knuckles on her hips and said, "No fishing if I don't see you by the count of three! One, two . . ."

"Oh, let him stay," Mama chided. Virgil and Felix tumbled onto the gravel path. Felix was much taller than Virgil, and at nine, he looked closer to Therese's age. He used his long arms to try to snatch a strip of paper from Virgil's hand. Although he was smaller, Virgil was a year older, and too fast. He taunted Felix, dangling the paper just out of reach and then running away. Justine grabbed Virgil and kissed his grubby cheek. Felix sought refuge in Mama's arms.

"You mind Therese while I'm gone. No running off. I heard The General's men were in the dark woods," Justine warned.

"If I saw The General, I'd kick him in the balls. And running away from Therese is too easy anyway!" Virgil laughed, sprinting off down the path. Felix and Therese gave chase, kicking up more dust. Mama and Justine continued down the path to the lake, where it met the Long Road. They would have to walk quickly to get to market before the stalls opened. Mr. Muhangi hummed as he held his fishing pole. He waved a bony hand in greeting from his red rowboat.

"Any luck, Mr. Muhangi?" Mama called out. He pulled a string of flat, silver fish from the water. His eyes nearly disappeared into his wrinkles when he smiled.

"God is good," he bragged. And why shouldn't he brag? When The Volcano was quiet, when the rains were bountiful, when the lake was still, the village prospered. The cassava and bananas that

Luna and Justine grew sold well at the market. Their children minded their parents and kept away from the dark woods.

Mama and Justine continued down the Long Road. Justine stopped to adjust her load again. She sighed, "If God is so good, why do women have to carry these baskets?" and Mama clapped her hands once and opened them toward Heaven, as if to say, "Only God knows."

"Soon you'll have Therese to help you," Justine said. Mama didn't want her daughter to ever have to carry baskets to market. As if reading her mind, Justine continued, "You can't keep her a child forever. Soon, even her Sunday dress won't be enough to hide the young woman she's becoming."

On Saturday morning, nobody worried about whether Felix and Virgil were ready for school, or if the chickens were fed. The children laughed, and the weaver birds wheezed and went tat-tat in the trees all morning. The only other sounds were Papa's hammer as it struck the thatched roof and Mr. Muhangi's humming. When the birds stopped singing, Virgil peeked from his hiding place to see an army of men pouring out of the dark woods.

CHAPTER TWO

~~~~~~~~~~

Virgil crawled out from his hiding place between the cassava plants and shook Therese gently. He tugged down her dress because he didn't want to see the blood from what happened to her. She didn't move. His knees were sore from crouching so long in the field. He shook her again, and her eyes fluttered open.

"We need to go, Therese, before the men with the guns find us."

He grabbed her hand. She struggled to her feet like a baby goat. He pulled her out of the cassava field toward the dark woods that their parents told them were not safe. Behind the children, in the golden sun, smoke rose from their village. It was not from their cook fire.

Therese shook as she ran up the wet, slippery hill. *Pole pole*, step by step, struggling to keep up with Virgil. The sun dipped, dimming their final steps to the forest. At the edge of the trees, screaming and gunfire reached their ears. Therese could not clear the smoke in her head, and she sat down, harder than she meant to. It hurt a lot. Virgil had made it to the top of the hill without fighting for breath. He was not even winded. Although he was only ten, he was the fastest in the village. The best soccer player. The cleverest at catching fish. His papa, Father Alexandre, was the priest at the Protestant church on the Long Road and demanded excellence of him. His papa and her papa both would scold them for being out after dark.

"We need to go back, Virgil. Our parents will be angry. We need to go home."

He swatted at her as if she were an irritating mosquito, even though she was older by almost two years. He leaned in close and hissed in Swahili, "Don't you see, Therese? There's no home now."

She looked down at their village and saw smoke rising high against the evening sky. Until that moment, she had never been afraid of anything. She felt abandoned by nearly everybody.

"Where is Felix? Is my little brother still playing in the cassava field? Is he hiding from the bad men?" she thought. She put her hand to her cheek. The skin was rough, like a pineapple. She looked down at herself. Her favorite Sunday dress was ruined. Therese stood. Wetness poured out of her and made a puddle at her feet.

"Why do I hurt so much there?" she wondered. Blood soaked through the green fabric. She held her hands in front of the bloody dress and felt a piece of paper in her front pocket. She unfolded the scrap and found Felix's message. It was written in English, the language Mama gave them.

I am here. Felix.

And then she remembered. And she fell down into a merciful blackness.

—⚏—

Virgil woke her again. It was dark and she could see only the whites of his eyes and his rumpled white shirt.

"We're still too close," he whispered. "The bad men might find us. We must go deeper into the woods." The crumpled paper was still in her hand. She tried to stand, but her legs would not carry her. She crawled after him. Virgil hardly made a sound as his small form disappeared among the trees.

The remembered thing lived in her head, on her cheek, and between her legs.

She and the boys had been playing treasure hunt, a game like hide-and-seek, in their parents' fields. Virgil always played with Therese and Felix. He didn't have any brothers or sisters, so they called him their "unbrother" ever since she could remember. She would sneak off, leaving the boys little clues about her location. On scraps of the stationery she had gotten for Christmas a few weeks before, she wrote *in the big tree*, or *under the pier*, or *near the Long Road*, and the boys would follow her trail until they found her. When it was Felix's turn, he wrote *I am here* because he was only nine and didn't really understand how to play.

Earlier Mama had taken the manioc flour to the market. It was almost time for Therese to draw water from the lake.

As her knee scraped against a tree root, she remembered more.

When they heard gunfire from the village, the boys were hiding in the cassava field. Therese started to run to find them, but before she got off the road, a man in military khaki pants and a black T-shirt grabbed her and hit her with his gun. He pulled up her favorite dress. She kicked him and screamed. He put his hand around her neck, and she kicked him off. He hit her again with his gun. She went limp. She looked up to see Papa running toward her, calling, "Felix! Therese!"

The man with the gun aimed at Papa and shot him in the leg. Two other men in uniforms, busy pouring gasoline on a hut, stopped what they were doing and fell on him with machetes. They cut her papa into pieces. As she watched, the man caused hot pain between her legs. The last thing she remembered was Felix running to stop the thing happening to their papa. A uniformed man grabbed Felix and put him face down in what was once their father, holding him there, laughing.

She crawled on the ground and moaned like an animal because that was what she remembered. The paper in her hand held her little brother's round scrawl in the English that their mama spoke to them. Therese heard a keening sound reverberating through the woods. Where was he? Where was Felix?

"Hush, Therese!" Virgil pulled her behind a tree. He crouched down and put his skinny arms around her tight. She cried and cried. She was eleven, their mothers had told her to look after Virgil and Felix, but he held her as though she were a baby. She was ashamed. Ashamed for not being fast like Virgil. Ashamed for being weak. Ashamed for what the man had done to her.

She clawed the ground and pushed the dirt into her face. She cried to him, "Where is Felix?"

"They took him," he whispered.

—⟋⟍—

They climbed deeper into the woods. A light rain fell. It felt strange to Therese, hiding with Virgil and not having Felix come find them. This was not a child's game any longer. The night closed in on the woods and was thick with damp heat and mosquitoes. Virgil swatted at a mosquito buzzing near his ear.

"If we had a cook fire, the smoke would chase them away," said Therese. She watched a whelp swell on her leg. Mosquitoes always found her. "And we need to find our families." She wondered if Mama knew what happened in the village.

"We can't risk a fire. The bad men might see it," he said.

Her tears began again, and she used her fists to push them away. It was hard to focus on what they needed when she made lakes on the ground with her tears. Virgil sat near her. He let her cry for both of them. What happened to his family? She could not ask him. He would have his own remembered things.

—⟋⟍—

Therese awoke in the middle of the night, shivering in her wet dress. Always after their meal and cleaning, her family and she would lie together in their bed. Sometimes it would get too hot, but never too cold. Outside, on the hill, in the woods, it was so cold that even the mosquitoes found someplace else to sleep.

Virgil refused to lie near her. He was not her brother, and he slept away from her. Like his papa, he had always been stubborn. He shivered in his sleep. Therese went to him and lay down, trying to warm him. She was lucky he was with her. She promised herself not to let her tears blind her to this anymore.

As the lazy sun woke over the hills beyond and dried the fog that settled in the valley overnight, she could see that they were just above the market. In the near light, she saw the outline of the central town. Crazed with sadness, pain, and fear, she had not realized that Virgil had been leading her to find their mamas at the market.

"Your face looks bad," Virgil muttered, still half asleep. He sat up and stretched.

"You always say that," she reminded him, turning away. He was always teasing her. But she knew he was right. Her cheek throbbed, and her swollen eye did not want to open.

He hid behind a tree to make water. Therese found her own tree and leaned against it. Her water came out slowly and at a funny angle. Something was not right with her down there. The river of wetness had stopped, replaced by swelling and burning. She didn't mention it to Virgil. He was a boy and would not understand. She wanted Mama to explain all of this and to tell her what to do. Tugging her dress down, she stood.

"How do we know the bad men aren't in the market too?" she whispered to Virgil.

"We don't, but it's so early. No one is moving. We'll be the only ones awake there."

They walked through the trees, and she wished one of them had a machete. They would have to climb down through wet tangles of bush to get back to the road. They made their way down the hillside, staying low, trying not to fall in the mud. They moved so slowly that the tops of the plants hardly wiggled. Still anyone could see them, if they were looking.

The cane fields met up with the bottom of the hill. At least if they couldn't make it to the market, they could chew on some sugar cane. Therese was suddenly so hungry that she could not focus on finding Mama. Virgil had been to market with his mama many times. He knew just where to go. They followed a small creek that ran down through a trough in the hillside and cut its way through the cane field.

At the edge of the field, they stopped. Therese heard a sound coming from just beyond the field but could not see through the stalks. The unseen thing snorted. Virgil heard it, too, and he put his finger to his lips. They only moved their eyeballs. Was it another bad man with a gun? Her heart, cheek, and the pain between her legs all throbbed together, and she heard the sound again. Therese's eyes strained in the half-light.

Suddenly a baby pig stepped out into the river for a drink. Virgil and Therese let out the breath that they'd been holding. Perhaps the pig brought good news. Possibly the bad men had not taken everything. Surely they would have taken the piglet. Or maybe, like the children, it was hiding. Therese listened for the greater grumble of its mother, but did not hear her, and she felt sorry for the little pig, all alone in the sugar cane field.

Virgil crept along the ground toward the market. Therese followed close behind. Around the hillside's curve sat the clearing where local villagers met to sell and buy what they needed. Their mamas always brought manioc flour and fruit in the afternoons. As they came around into the clearing, they heard it—the hiss of a radio. A man talked into it. They could not understand what language he spoke. Was it one of the bad men with guns? Was it a soldier? Virgil froze. Something wasn't right. Cassava leaves, fish, bananas were everywhere. There were no familiar brown faces, only men wearing blue helmets that glinted in the early light. The Blue Head men! Maybe they had driven the bad men away! The pavement was empty but for the UN peacekeepers' three big MONUSCO trucks. Virgil stood tall and ran toward them. Therese limped along behind him, trying to hold her head up.

A funny smell made its way to her. Six of the UN Blue Heads passed a small cigarette to one another and lounged under the overhang of the banana sellers' lean-tos. One squat Blue Head noticed an unharmed banana, pulled it from a basket, and threw it to his friend. It hit the other Blue Head in the ear, and he jumped to his feet, gibbering in a funny tongue. Therese did an inventory of the languages Mama taught Felix and her: Swahili, French, English. The man wasn't speaking any of them. He had a thick, black mustache that curled around his lips. He looked a little familiar. She thought she had seen him near their lake. All the other Blue Heads jumped to their feet when they caught sight of them. They stared hard, as if African children were the last thing they would expect to see in Congo. The squat Blue Head stubbed out the cigarette. She summoned her best French.

"Please, help us!" she begged of the squat man. He looked confused and shook his head. He turned to the man with the black mustache who held the banana.

"Hey, teacher's daughter, do you speak English?" the mustache man asked. His eyes were red, and Therese did not trust him. He stared at her bloody dress. She crossed her hands in front of herself.

"I do," she said and pointed at Virgil. "You are eating his family's bananas."

Therese stared back at him, wondering what happened. Did he and his Blue Head friends not notice the overturned baskets? The broken eggs? The tracks of blood? The mustache man hid the banana behind his back. He asked her where her family was. Therese didn't know what to tell him. Another Blue Head yelled into a radio. Virgil, silent until then, started to talk. His remembered things flowed from his mouth in Swahili. She translated for him.

"The bad men, they came over the hill in the afternoon. We were playing in the cassava fields. They caught my friend and took him and made him do bad things!"

Therese whipped her head around and stopped her translation. Virgil went on, "They took my friend's sister . . ." he gestured at her dress and at her pain. She felt a rage building. It was not his place to tell these men what happened to her in the field. The Blue Heads stared at her, expecting a translation. But she would not give it. She clapped her hands once and opened them to Heaven before her.

"My village has been burned and the people have been taken away or killed," Therese said angrily. "Where were you yesterday? Where are our mamas? They were supposed to be here!"

The mustache man talked to the Blue Head holding the radio. He asked questions in a bubbly, Asian-sounding tongue. Therese tried to remember the Asian countries. China, Japan, India, Pakistan. The radio man nodded his head. Therese turned to Virgil, but he had gone into the market to look for his mother. He ran from stall to stall, flipping over baskets and blankets. The red-eyed mustache man turned to Therese.

"We'll take you to The City for medical treatment," he said. "You can talk to the authorities about what happened to your village." His head bobbled from side to side, as if it were a little bit loose. He smiled at her as though this were the right answer, as if what he was telling her would make everything okay.

It seemed like the mustache man had not heard her. Did he not understand that a whole village was burned, and her papa was chopped with a machete? She did not want medical treatment. She wanted her family. She wanted her mama. Why was he just sitting there with the others when so many had been hurt nearby?

"What about my brother? What about my mother? Can you use your trucks and guns and go find the people who did this? Why do you not help us?" Therese demanded, pointing at Virgil.

Among the ruined stalls, Virgil shook his head "no," and sank to his knees. He was studying something on the ground. Therese's legs hardly carried her. She was almost too hungry and wobbly to get to him. The Blue Head men spoke in their bubbling language behind her, but she tried to ignore them. Virgil crouched over what used to be Justine's blanket. He reached for what looked like dried manioc, but the pieces were too small. He held one in his palm. It was a tooth. Therese knelt beside him. There were many more teeth on his mama's blanket and in the dirt. Blood too. Virgil's eyes were unblinking. His remembered things seemed to be speaking to him. Before she could stop him, he put the tooth on his tongue and swallowed it.

"No, Virgil!" she cried. He already had another handful of teeth near his lips. She grabbed his wrist. The Blue Head men rushed up to them.

"Mama! Mama!" screamed Virgil. He scrambled around, collecting teeth. The mustache man pulled Virgil away from the blanket.

"What is he doing? Why is he eating pig's teeth?" Therese demanded. She tried to get to her feet, but the ground swayed under her and she fell. The Blue Heads stood over her, and everything looked as if she were underwater. She felt herself being wrapped in a blanket and lifted up.

They sat in the Blue Heads' cold MONUSCO trucks. Therese had been in a bus before, but this was different. The inside was clean and new. It was as big as her family's hut. Cold air rushed from a vent in the door, and her dress became clammy on her skin. She shivered next to Virgil, who cried and cried. The Blue Head men wrapped him in a blanket too. The mustache man said, "Buckle up," but she did not know what that meant until he reached over and strapped a seat belt over her. They were given bottles of clean water and candy bars. Every time Therese had seen Blue Head men, they offered candy.

Months earlier, they had come with some businessmen to the village and gone down to the lake. Ever since Therese was a baby, and even before she was born, children in their village believed there was a giant fish making bubbles in the lake. Felix and Therese would sit by the lake and watch the bubbles rise to the surface. Virgil would sit with them sometimes, trying to catch a look at the giant. Mama had said for years that people from around the world would come there. As soon as Felix and Therese started saying words, she began schooling them in proper French and English, so that when white people came to visit their lake, they would be able to communicate with them. Mama was lucky. She grew up in

The City before the Rwandan genocide and got to attend school. All the classes were taught in French, and she also studied English. She and Papa met while he was studying to be a teacher at the university in The City. When refugees flowed over the border into The City fifteen years earlier, Mama and Papa moved to their home on the lake.

When Therese got older, she learned what Mama already knew—that it was really the methane gas making the bubbles, and not a fish at all. Mama explained that a mountain at the bottom of the lake was continually leaking natural gases to the surface, and Papa added that the gas could power Congo for generations. Soon the white men paved the highway to the village so they could explore the lake. Therese spoke three languages. Because she could read English and French, she always felt connected to other parts of the world. She dreamed of traveling to America, England, and France. Now she only wanted to be home with Mama, Papa, and Felix.

Therese shivered in her blanket. Her candy was so sweet. The chocolate taste she remembered from when the foreign men in business suits came with MONUSCO's Blue Heads to their village. They handed out the same candy bars. She thought hard about that. If the Blue Head men knew where the village was, and the market, why did they not help when the bad men came? Did the bad men follow them? Was that how they knew about the village?

Virgil was quiet. He ate the candy like the starving child he was. Therese crumpled her candy wrapper and they pulled away from the market. As the lead truck rolled in the direction of The City, she noticed more red smears on the ground. Someone had written in blood on the pavement in large letters the word "FELIX."

She grabbed Virgil's arm and pointed. They rolled over the letters, and Virgil and Therese strained to get a look out the rear window. They were going in the wrong direction, away from Mama and Felix.

"We cannot leave!" she blurted to the mustache man, "There are still survivors with the bad men! They took my mama and brother!"

"We'll return to the market with the army," the Blue Head said. "We'll survey the damage to your village. Right now, you need a doctor, and so does he."

She looked at Virgil. He was so young. He had seen terrible things. So had she. They could jump out of the truck right now. They could go and look for their families. Instead they were going to tell their story so that someone else could find them. She turned around again and looked out the window. Therese could hardly see the market anymore, and then it disappeared around the bend. She was cold and hungry and hurt, and she felt there was nothing she could do. The road was smooth, and the rocking of the truck calmed her. She curled up under her blanket and rested her head on the window. Virgil was already asleep. She thought about the brave little piglet searching for its mother, while she sat in a fancy truck eating chocolate. She felt ashamed again.

CHAPTER THREE

~~~~~~~~~~~~

Therese awoke when her head bumped against the truck's window. As they approached The City, the smooth road gave way to a series of wide potholed paths, which seemed to lead nowhere. The air was dusty and smoky, as if someone had lit a cook fire and thrown dirt on it only moments ago. She cleared her throat, but it tasted like the smoke from The City's air would never leave the inside of her mouth. There were people dressed in Western clothes everywhere. They were very smart in their business suits and high-heeled shoes. She looked down at her dirty dress. Virgil already noticed that city people wore closed shoes. He wiggled his toes in his dusty flip-flops.

The driver swerved to avoid a boy on a bicycle and nearly ran over a mama and her baby. The jerry can on the mama's head hardly moved as she stepped out of the way. The baby on her back stared at them through the window.

One time, when Papa met with a French church group that was visiting Therese's village, he took her in their bus to The City. They went to a big, white building and saw all the *mzungu* people handing out schoolbooks to the Africans. The room was tidy, with a solid, concrete floor, and even though there were hundreds of people there, everything was in order, all lined up. As they made their way through the hospital's giant gate, Therese noticed the same thing. The parking lot held many vehicles, all lined up. The hospital compound was protected by a volcanic rock wall with barbed wire on top. The gate closed behind them, and for the first time in two days, Therese felt safe. As if no bad men could get to her there.

When they got out of the truck, the Blue Head men brought them into a big room. After sitting so long, Therese found it hard to walk. The pain between her legs was still very great. She noticed the lights overhead. They were so bright they hurt her eyes.

"Where's the generator?" asked Virgil, reading her mind. Therese asked the man with the twisty mustache, and he smiled at her.

"No generator here. Just real electricity," he explained. He pointed to some chairs, and Virgil and she sat. The cool plastic felt strange against the backs of Therese's legs. The hospital's entrance was quite cheerful, with colorful paintings on the walls and desks under large windows. Two village women in brilliantly colored wraps and headscarves sat and typed at a computer. Virgil pointed at what he called "the magical box" because he had never seen a computer before. Therese did not care about the glowing screen; she strained to see the women's faces. Neither one was her mama or his, and neither was from their village. One woman looked at her and smiled in a sad way. Therese turned away from her eyes and looked down at her bloody dress.

A nurse in a clean, white uniform glided toward them. Her brown skin stood out against her clothes. Her name tag said Desanges, which in French meant "the angels." She knelt before Therese. She glanced at Therese's dress and at her cheek. Therese thought she smelled like flowers. Her French was lovely.

"Can you walk?" she asked Therese.

"Yes. Slowly." Therese pointed at Virgil. "And so can he."

"Is he injured?" the nurse asked.

"Just by what he saw," Therese answered.

Even though Virgil went to school and the classes were taught in French, his family never practiced the language with him the way Therese's mama did with her. He spoke to the nurse in Swahili.

"Please let me stay with Therese."

Surprisingly she answered him in Swahili. Maybe the nurse was from Congo also.

"We need to help Therese with her injuries, but you may come with us and wait outside the examining room," she said.

Therese glanced back to the mustache man, who waved good-bye to her. A large Congolese man in a white uniform and a name tag that said "Valentin" arrived with a rolling chair. He said he was there to give her a ride and gestured for her to sit. Virgil laughed a bit to see Therese rolled across the floor and out the back door. He walked next to her rolling chair and down a ramp. Behind the building was a courtyard. It looked like a little village. There was an area where women washed and dried clothes in the sunshine. There was also a cook fire area and a place to prepare food. There was even a playground with swings. Therese looked at Virgil, and he pointed to the climbing structure. The flower-smelling angel nurse walked beside them with a clipboard.

Valentin pushed Therese into a building marked "Family Planning," and she wondered about the name. Perhaps all the children who were planning to see their families again went there. Desanges put her arm around Virgil, and Therese was rolled through the door. In the lobby sat an elderly woman, probably a *nyanya*, a grandma, holding a newborn baby who cried a lot. The *nyanya* loosened her shirt from her *kanga* and put the baby to her breast. Was it possible the old woman was the baby's mother?

Therese was rolled past the Family Planning desk and down a hallway. Two older girls passed her. They may have been thirteen or fourteen and they carried babies in their bellies. Therese understood why she was there. She turned to Desanges and addressed her in French.

"Miss! There must be some mistake. All of the women in here have babies."

Virgil looked confused, but Therese ignored his face. He would not understand.

"I am too young to have a baby. I have not started my periods."

The nurse said, "Really?" and moved on quickly. "We need to hear what the soldiers did to you. We have to examine you to make sure your insides aren't hurt. If you have injuries, we'll fix them. This is where we do the check-ups on all the girls and women."

Valentin stopped the rolling chair and gestured for Virgil to wait on a bench. Virgil did not want to be left alone and he started to whine.

"I don't want to stay here. I want to go with Therese!" he cried. Finally, in Swahili, Valentin spoke. His voice was deep and rumbly, like thunder over the mountain.

"Little brother, I've been through some hard times too. We'll share stories. I'll sit with you." He smiled at Virgil and perched on the bench.

"What have you seen?" asked Virgil. Valentin seemed not so big now. He rolled up his sleeve and showed them a tattoo. It was a skull with two machine guns crossing over it. Virgil looked at Therese, and she nodded. He sat next to Valentin and reached out to touch the tattoo. Valentin seemed like a man who would take care of Therese's little unbrother.

Desanges walked her into an examination room. She handed Therese a bag for her clothes and a little white half-dress with flowers on it. She pointed to a corner of the room where Therese changed behind a screen. The half-dress smelled like soap as Therese slipped it over her shoulders, and she remembered how dirty she was. Her backside was cold and bare, and she did not want to come out from behind the screen.

"It's okay. I won't look," Desanges said. Therese came out holding her bag in one hand and the back of her gown together in the other. Desanges looked so clean in her white dress, and Therese felt ashamed and she stared at the floor.

"On the counter is a cup. Can you go in the bathroom and pee into it?" she asked.

The bathroom was beautiful and shiny and had an above-ground toilet with water in it. At her village, they used an outhouse with a hole in the ground. The last time she used a real bathroom was when she helped Papa pick up school supplies for the boys' school a few weeks earlier. When she had stood on the seat, a lady yelled at her because she'd left footprints. "Stupid girl, you don't stand on it, you sit!" At least she knew better then. As Therese peed into the cup, she thought about Papa. She thought about what a good teacher he was and how he helped so many boys in the village. Why did the bad men come to kill him? Why did they take her brother? Where was Felix? Where was Mama? Her legs started to tremble, and then she was shaking all over. Therese did not realize she was groaning until Desanges said, "Are you okay, Therese?"

She put her cup down and went out. Therese could not stay there, and she told the nurse as much.

"I know," she sighed.

"I need to find my family." Therese begged her.

"Therese, you're sick with fever and injuries. You can't go anywhere until you're well."

She gestured to an exam table, and Therese sat, grateful for something solid beneath her legs. The paper crinkled under her.

"The doctor will be here soon. Can you tell me what happened?"

Therese looked at the nurse and wondered if she grew up in a village like her own. How did she get to go to school, when Therese did not? Therese liked her because she was beautiful and smelled good in her white dress. She wore a pin with an angel on it. Therese told her story.

Several days later, Therese's wounds were getting better. The head doctor was a kind Congolese man named Dr. Bingi. He gave Therese medicine for the fever and stitched the wounds in her sex while she slept. He said she was lucky. Therese was not carrying any illness that would stay with her. Her cheek was healing too. The bad man's gun did not break her cheekbone. Dr. Bingi said the stitches on her cheek would fade to a thin scar.

Virgil stayed in the boys' wing of the hospital. Although his body was ready for fishing again, his mind was hurt from what he'd seen in the market. He and Therese saw each other at meals, in the courtyard, and they whispered of finding their mamas and Felix.

Therese's roommate was a girl named Odette. She was hurt by bad men too. She was dragged around from village to village and made to have sex with them for months. She was pregnant, with two babies. She was only a year older than Therese, and already, her parts were broken. Her twins would come soon. Her papa beat her when she tried to go home with the bad men's babies inside her, so she would have the babies there. Dr. Bingi would take the babies from her belly as one might open a passion fruit and pull out the insides. Odette told Therese that she was not so lucky. While Odette would get to have her babies there and live at the hospital for a while, Therese would have no place to go. Therese thought they were both lucky to be alive, but unlucky because they were away from their families.

Therese met a *mzungu,* a white woman, called Amy, who came to the hospital often. She had hair the color of fire. Behind her glasses, her blue eyes squinted shut when she listened to the children talk about the families they lost. She asked Therese many questions about her family and village. Therese did not want to talk to her at first but was curious about her orange-colored hair. She asked her why she didn't have to shave her head in order to stay clean, like the children in her village. The *mzungu's* hair was long and curly, and a color Therese had never seen. Amy said, "Let's take turns. I ask a question, and then you ask one. Deal?" She extended her hand to Therese. They shook on it. Amy asked Therese to list the people who lived with her before the attack. She had spoken to Virgil too.

The way Amy spoke to Therese made her think Virgil and she would not be there long. She said things like, "I bet you'd love to get out of here." But Papa was gone, and Mama was missing, and Therese felt like she was an orphan. Virgil was like an orphan too. When Therese mentioned it to Odette, she said that if they were orphans, someone would likely take them away to an orphanage far from there. Therese felt more and more nervous about that. If she moved from The City, she'd be farther from home. How would she find where Mama and Felix were taken? Therese wondered about Odette's twins. If they only had a mama, would they also go to the orphanage? Therese could not bring herself to ask.

—ᴍ—

Dr. Bingi examined her and said, "The stitches on your cheek dissolved and have fallen away. The stitches in your vagina have done the same."

Therese looked away. He continued, "Have you been taking the pills each day? They will take away the infection the bad man put in you."

Therese didn't mind being in the hospital. She and Virgil ate three meals each day, and nobody went hungry there.

Once a day, all the children who did not have babies got together with Dr. Bingi, and they talked about their hurt and what they would do next. The doctor reminded Therese of Papa a little. He gave good advice, like a teacher. And for someone who had seen much pain, he smiled a lot. When he heard a hard story about a child, his big hands clasped each other like he was praying. Papa had big hands too.

When Therese first arrived, Desanges explained that everyone had a job in the little village in the hospital. The girls and women made the food in the courtyard. The boys brought charcoal to make cook fires and they cleaned up after the morning meal. In the afternoon, the kids who would be leaving soon usually had time on the playground, while the ones who were staying longer went to classes at the hospital. The older girls went to the crafts center to sew, or the tech center, where they learned how to use computers. Virgil and Therese went to the playground, which meant they would be leaving soon. Therese wished she could learn in the classroom or in the tech center. But then she remembered Felix and Mama and felt terrible for wanting to stay.

One afternoon, Virgil and Therese were on the swings when she heard whispering on the playground. A slave boy had been brought to the hospital from the mines. This did not surprise Therese. Bad men took lots of children from villages in the area. Valentin told her unbrother that the boys were put to work mining coltan to be sold to international companies. She continued swinging, until a boy about Virgil's age ran up with new information about the slave boy from the mines. Virgil's eyes lit up.

"He says the new boy was taken to the mines from our market. It was the same day our mamas disappeared!"

Therese jumped off the swing. When she hit the ground, she felt it through her feet, ankles, and knees. She stood up strong for the first time in two weeks. Maybe this miner boy knew something about her family.

That evening, after the nighttime meal, Therese asked Odette about leaving. They always walked back to their room together. Odette waddled like a duck, with her belly swinging.

"Usually Desanges and Dr. Bingi go with the patients when they return to their towns and families," she said. "Lots of girls come back to the hospital after being raped and beaten again. Then they're moved to another place. Sometimes that works and sometimes not."

"Why can't they go back to their families?" asked Therese. The mosquitoes were out, and they crossed from the kitchen to their dorm room quickly.

"After you've carried the baby of the devil, husbands are not so forgiving, and their families are no better," Odette said. She swatted a mosquito on her arm. Therese held their door open for her. Odette went in to find the light switch. Therese was still not used to having electricity, and it surprised her again when the lights came on, showing their big, clean room with all the wood furniture, the dressers, the desks, and the colorful tapestries over the windows. It was the first space Therese did not have to share with her family. Instead of three roommates, she only had one. The room had two separate beds in it. Odette groaned as she plopped onto hers. Therese perched next to her and put her hand on Odette's belly. One of the babies kicked her hand.

"But what about Dr. Bingi and Amy?" Therese asked. "What about Desanges and Valentin? They can't take care of us forever. Don't they want us to go home?"

"Only if we have one," said Odette.

CHAPTER FOUR

~~~~~~~~~~

Dr. Bingi had told Odette that her babies would be a boy and a girl. It was confusing to Therese how he knew this. Therese touched Odette's belly and only felt movement. Odette said Dr. Bingi could see inside her with a machine. This made Therese nervous, imagining what kind of machine made pictures of a baby from the outside. Odette told her that the donated machine came from America. She said all the best things in Congo come from someplace else. Therese thought of all the books written by people in other places that her father brought home for Felix and her.

Odette and Therese passed the night trying to name her baby girl. Therese thought a name like Jane was good. It reminded her of Jane Eyre, a strong English girl in a book her mother gave her. Odette wanted an English name, although many Congolese girls' names were French. Therese was French. Odette was French. Even Mama had a foreign name: Luna. As Therese threw out ideas for Odette, she thought about Mama. Then she thought about the boy who was taken from the market and made to work in the mines. Could he help Therese find her family?

—⟶⟶—

The morning felt cool, and there was a cook fire going in the courtyard. The *nyanya* with the baby was always the first one up. Her name was Esther, and she could only see through one eye.

34

Both of her eyes, even the milky one, stared at Therese. She lifted charcoal logs onto her fire. Some cassava floated in a huge pot on the ground. Therese wondered how long she'd been awake. Her baby was so young he probably needed her early.

"Looking for the miner boy?" she asked.

"Yes. How did you know?" Therese shivered in the coolness of the early morning and pulled a fluffy Chicago Bears sweatshirt over her *kanga*.

"Virgil came by earlier."

Therese looked around the deserted playground and asked her where he went.

"Off to the recovery room," she said and gestured to the far building. "But they turned him away. The miner boy is quite sick and can't be bothered."

She straightened up and stretched. The baby on her back stared at Therese when Esther bent for more charcoal. Therese stooped to help her. Esther looked at Therese and cautioned, "Once you get out of here, remember that the roads are not safe at night. Stick to the woods when it's dark."

Therese did not know where Esther thought Therese would go, even if she could get out. Esther said, "That's how I got this one." She turned her back to Therese so she could see her baby's huge, owly eyes. "On the road at night."

Virgil shuffled up and slouched by the fire. He looked tired and troubled, as if he had been busy that morning.

"Boy, get up and help us," Esther said. He jumped up and hoisted the heavy pot onto the fire. He looked at his feet, ashamed for his selfishness.

"Sorry. I was thinking about the miner boy. If he dies, we won't know where to look for our families," he said.

Esther fixed her good eye on him. She said, "If God takes him, it will be a blessing. The mines are torture. If you think you've seen pain, you're wrong. You have not seen pain until you've been a slave there."

Therese wanted to ask how she knew that, but she was a bit afraid of her, so she said nothing.

The cooking vegetables smelled good, and Therese's stomach growled, wondering if she was going to feed it. The whole hospital seemed to be awake now that everyone smelled food. People emerged from their rooms and headed to the kitchen. Incredibly, this early in the day, Therese saw Amy. Her wild, red hair stood out against the drab, smoky air. She carried a large microphone on a long stick and was with a tall, skinny white man with a camera. He chomped chewing gum with his mouth open, like a cow. They were moving quickly toward the recovery room. The shirts on their backs said FREE CHILD SLAVES. They must have been there for the miner boy. Therese wondered where Dr. Bingi was. He seemed never to sleep. Therese strained to look through the growing crowd, but she could not see him, so she followed Virgil to the kitchen to help with the morning meal.

Later in the afternoon, Odette and Therese spotted Virgil on the playground in the courtyard. He bumped his fist against an older boy's. Although the boy looked to be no more than fourteen, he had a tattoo on his arm, just like Valentin's, a skull with crossed machine guns over it like crossbones. As he turned, Therese saw that the tattooed boy had only one leg. He was so graceful on the one foot that she hardly noticed that he was missing the other. He leaned lightly on a cane and smiled at her with teeth as bright as the lobby lights.

"This is Robert," said Virgil.

"Hi," Odette and Therese said. Therese's voice squeaked and sounded funny to herself. Therese's knees felt a bit shaky. Robert was a handsome boy. He grinned at her.

"He came here with his brother, Jacques, the miner boy who is in recovery," Virgil explained. "We're sorry to hear your brother has been hurt. Right, Therese?" He elbowed her, oblivious to her reaction to Robert.

Robert ignored him and asked, "Do you need information about a child in the mines or a boy in the ranks?"

"Both," said Virgil, as Therese opened her mouth.

"I'll tell you what I know, but you have to give me something I can work with," said Robert, squinting at us and running his tongue over his teeth.

Therese felt a little strange, telling this boy that she showed up there at the hospital with only Virgil and the clothes on her body. She had nothing to give him.

"About two hours from here on the highway is our village," Virgil began.

As her unbrother told what happened to them, she realized that because Robert was the miner boy's brother, he was looking for someone too. He asked a lot of questions about the man who attacked her. Therese wondered why he needed to know. Was he looking for the men who kidnapped his brother? It did not matter because she could not remember what her attacker looked like. Her head held the events of that day, but not the face of the bad man. Robert asked about the men who killed her papa and burned the house down. Therese could not give him that either. Even though she had told the few things she knew to Dr. Bingi and Amy, she felt ashamed to tell Robert that she remembered almost nothing that could help him.

Virgil and Therese had told their story to so many people in group meetings that they had gotten very good at some of the details, but they still left some out too. Like how the man who raped her wore a necklace of human teeth. And how Virgil saw a bad man pull the trigger on the gun that shot Papa as he ran toward her. And Virgil never mentioned that he was attacked and almost raped too. These things they talked about when they were alone. The boy soldier, Robert, seemed interested in their story, but he did not ask any more questions. He must have had his own remembered things.

"When I visit my brother, I'll ask him about your families," he told them. "There's a very bad man at the head of the militia group. They call him The General. He is hired by international business-people to take out villages, plunder, and claim land. His brother is the head of the mine. He is known as The Mole. They have an operation where they work together to bring down our villages by taking the women and children."

"How do you know all of this?" Therese asked. She felt strange about the boy. Although he was handsome and interesting, Therese did not trust him completely. He pointed to his tattoo.

"They took my brother to the mines, and I was forced into the militia." He smiled his perfect smile at her and licked his teeth again. "But I got out." Therese wondered about how he lost his leg. She wanted to ask him how he escaped the bad men, but she didn't.

"Will you tell us how to find our families?" Virgil asked.

"You don't need to go looking for them," Robert said. "You should stay where you are and talk to Free Child Slaves. They can help, if you know how to talk to them."

"But while we're healing in here, our families are out there dying, being tortured . . ." she argued. Therese did not care how handsome the older boy was because she did not agree with him. He just smiled with those perfect teeth and looked at her.

"What good are you if you're dead too? Free Child Slaves came in with the UN to get me out of the ranks. Let them do their job."

"What good are we in here?" Therese threw her arms in the air.

"Use your time in here to learn English, computers, farming," he said. "You may find that when you get out, you're the only one of your family left." She looked at him and realized that he had seen so much more than she had. He was right, but they only taught computers and crafts to people who were staying longer than she.

"I already speak English, but how can that help?" Therese asked.

"If you speak like a *mzungu*, you have a gift," Robert said. "Don't forget you have it. White people love to document suffering with their cameras and microphones. Tell them your story in

English and you'll be out of here before you know it." He winked at her.

Desanges appeared at Therese's side. Her beautiful face looked crumpled, like a stepped-on flower. She was very serious as she put her arm around Robert and led him away. Therese felt sad that she did not have a chance to thank him for his advice.

"I hope his brother gets better," Virgil said with a sigh. Odette had been watching Therese like a mother. She gave her a nudge with her elbow and told her, "He's cute."

That night, Therese dreamt about her family. Papa, Mama, and Felix were fishing near the lake. Felix had a pile of fish at his feet, and Mama helped him put them into a basket. Mama and Felix started back to their house, while Papa stayed and watched bubbles rise to the surface of the lake. The giant fish jumped out of the water and swallowed him whole.

Therese woke up screaming, and Odette perched on the edge of her bed and grabbed her hand.

"I want to go home. I want my family back!" Therese cried. Odette petted her head and rubbed Therese's back.

"I know. I do too," she whispered.

Therese twisted in her blankets for a while, unable to sleep. After Odette had gone back to her snoring, Therese slipped from her bed. The floor was cold under her feet, and she was relieved to find her flip-flops. She shrugged a fleece over her nightgown and crept out the door. She followed the smell of a burning cigarette to the playground. Robert swung slowly back and forth in the shadows. They were alone in the courtyard, which made her both nervous and excited.

"Hi," she whispered, and he exhaled smoke from his mouth while inhaling it through his nose.

"I was hoping you'd come," Robert said. Therese rubbed her arms for warmth. She climbed onto the swing next to his. She was amazed he could balance on the swing using only one foot.

"Did The General do that to you?" she finally asked him.

He squinted through the smoke and said, "I don't know. I was guarding the coltan mine one day, and saw my brother being slapped by another guard. He was only putting down his shovel for a drink of water. I ran into the pit thinking I could save him. There was a gunshot, and a terrible pain in my leg."

Therese thought about what Robert had told her before—to stay safe and let Free Child Slaves find her family.

"How did Amy find you?" she asked.

"The General has no use for wounded soldiers, and he hates to waste bullets. The next transport truck out of the mine dumped me in the woods and left me to die. It took me two days to crawl to the road. Amy and Jeff were driving by with a UN escort, and they brought me here to Dr. Bingi. He had to amputate my leg because it was so infected."

"You're very brave," said Therese.

He shook his head like he did not believe her.

"Is your brother okay?" He shook his head again and shrugged his shoulders. The ash on his cigarette fell on the ground where his second foot should have been. He picked at his tongue and flicked away a stray bit of tobacco. "Why do people do this?' he asked. "Jacques is just a kid."

Therese had no answer for him. Even though Robert was older than she, even if he already smoked, he was also just a kid. She reached over and took his free hand.

They stayed like that for a good, long while. He was on his third cigarette when Valentin appeared. Therese recognized him in the dark because of his big shoulders. He exchanged an elaborate handshake with Robert that ended with each of them patting their tattoos.

Valentin told him, "You're going to get me fired, man. No smoking in the courtyard."

Robert dropped his cigarette, and Therese stomped on it for him.

He asked Valentin, "Any change yet?"

"No, but Dr. Bingi wants to see you." He helped Robert up and gave him his cane.

"Good luck," Therese said with a sigh.

Robert smiled sadly, and even in the dark, she could see his bright white teeth.

—w—

The next day went on forever. Robert had not returned from his brother Jacques's bedside. Neither had Amy, Desanges, or Dr. Bingi been seen in the courtyard. A rumor went around that Jacques was shot while trying to escape from the mining camp. His infections were raging, and he had been in a very deep sleep for days. Even Dr. Bingi could not wake him up.

Virgil drove Therese crazy, walking in circles. He asked a series of stupid questions.

"What if the miner boy dies?"

"Then Robert will be sad," she told him.

"What if Robert leaves and we never see him again?" Virgil asked. She clapped her hands once and opened them to Heaven. The truth was she did not want Robert to leave them any more than Virgil did. He saw Robert as a link to the outside world. Therese saw him as more. A special friend. A handsome, older, special friend.

In the evening, Therese took Virgil to talk to Esther. She would help them understand what would happen next. They found her nursing her baby near the playground.

"In the eyes of this hospital, you're either a head of family or an orphan," she explained. "If you're too old to be adopted, you'll probably go to an Internally Displaced People's camp. If you're young enough, the church that pays for the hospital will find you a home."

"But our families may still be alive," Therese protested. "We don't need new ones. We need to find ours."

Virgil was over arguing with anyone. His listened nervously, pacing back and forth.

"If your family is out there, you should take comfort that you're in here," Esther said. She swept her hand over the scene of playing children. They looked happy, pushing each other on the swings and kicking donated soccer balls.

Therese asked, "But what about you, Esther? Where will you go when your baby's old enough?"

"My family won't take me back," she said. "Nobody will. I'm too ugly with this baby and without my eye. Desanges has helped me to apply to transfer to a school called New Beginnings, where I can learn how to start a business of my own. I can learn self-defense, to fight off attackers. I can even go to university from there if I want. The application takes a long time, but God willing, I'll go soon."

"Can I go with you to New Beginnings?" asked Virgil.

"It's a place for women with no other options," Esther said. "You're a boy and you have options. If you can't find your family, someone will take you in."

"Do I have options?" Therese asked. She felt as if she were speaking with a fortune-teller, like the ones she read about in books. Esther seemed to have all the answers Therese needed. Esther gazed at her as if she were picturing Therese in other clothes. She squinted her good eye at her, while the other one stared milky and blue.

"Do you have any skills? Can you use a computer, farm, or sew?"

"I can read, speak, and write Swahili, French, and English," Therese said with pride.

"But can you make money doing that?" Esther asked. "If you plan to get out of here and survive, you need to have money of your own. And a home."

Virgil didn't have any skills of his own. He wasn't able to support himself any more than Therese was. And without parents to care for him, Therese was the only family Virgil had.

The conversation was making Virgil uneasy. He wrung his hands as he paced. Esther stared at him with her good eye. Her baby started to fuss, and she thrust him at Virgil. "As long as you're moving, make yourself useful!" she commanded.

Virgil took the baby. Put him on his shoulder and paced with him. The two seemed to calm each other. The baby stopped crying, and Virgil slowed down. He turned to Esther.

"Sometimes I think you're right: We should be happy that we're in here," he admitted.

Therese shook her head. "We can't stay here, Virgil. This place is for sick people, and we're not sick anymore. We need to talk to Amy about finding our families."

The baby fussed again, and Virgil handed him back to his mother.

"See you at group meeting tomorrow," he said over his shoulder and left.

"Watch that boy," Esther said as she put the baby back to her breast. "He's too nervous here."

CHAPTER FIVE

~~~~~~~~~~

That night Therese heard a loud crash and then crying in the courtyard. She opened her blinds and was surprised to see Virgil lying on his side near the climbing structure. In the lights around the playground, people ran from their rooms to where he was. Odette and Therese climbed from their beds. They got to the courtyard, just as Valentin and Desanges emerged in their robes, scraped Virgil off the ground, and helped him hobble to the medical ward. He continued to cry, but before he disappeared into the building, he looked over his shoulder at Therese, and she saw he was grinning through his tears. Odette and she followed him to the medical wing and strained to see through the window. Valentin helped Virgil into a rolling chair, and Desanges scribbled something on her clipboard.

"I wonder what happened," Therese said. Odette stared at her like she did not believe her.

"What happened was he found a way to stay here," she told her. "Virgil's not the first kid to jump off the climbing structure." Therese thought about this as they made their way back to their room. Had Virgil given up? Did he not want to find his family as much as Therese wanted to find her own? Therese felt alone in the fight to get out of the hospital.

—m—

Before the morning meal, Therese looked for Virgil. He had been released from medical. She found him on a chair beside Esther's cook fire. He looked comfortable with his foot propped up on a bench and Esther's sleeping baby in his arms. Somehow, she was not surprised to find him there. It was the cast that got her attention.

"So?" she asked. She knew what happened but was sure he had a story to tell her.

"I fell. It was an accident," he lied. "They say it's a hairline fracture. I'll be in this cast for weeks. Bad luck, right?"

"You're so stupid, Virgil. What if your family walked through the hospital gate right now? You can't play soccer. You won't be able to fish. You couldn't go to school. You'd have to stay home and read your Bible all day."

"My parents are gone," Virgil said, his eyes not meeting hers. "If they were alive, they would have found me here by now. I don't have a brother like you do. All I have is here at the hospital. I'm an orphan, like Esther says. You go out into the bush and find whoever you think is out there for you. I'm staying here as long as I can!"

The little baby started to whimper. Therese took him from Virgil and danced a bit with him. If he could, Virgil would have walked away from this conversation, but he was stuck. His crutches lay a few feet away from him on the ground. Therese nudged them away a little farther with her foot. The baby stared at her with his huge eyes.

"Where's Esther?" she asked.

"Off to find more charcoal. She's angry with me. She said I had options and now I have none."

"I don't agree with that. You have options. You can be a babysitter," Therese said. The baby was wet. She handed him back to Virgil, and he started crying again. Virgil twisted in his chair and held the little, soggy bundle away from himself. As Therese walked off, she was careful to kick the crutches even farther away.

—⁂—

Usually by then the courtyard was full of people looking for breakfast. That day, nobody was around. Therese made her way through the empty courtyard to the lobby of the hospital. Her stomach growled, but she had already made up her mind to skip breakfast. She felt like a caged animal. She needed answers, and she needed them immediately. When Therese arrived in the lobby, she could not believe what she saw. There was a huge line of patients in front of Amy, who sat at a folding table with Robert. The tall, skinny cameraman who arrived the day before focused his camera on them from the midst of the crowd. He still chomped his gum as though it were the best thing he ever tasted. Dozens of people must have decided to skip breakfast. Therese was amazed by all the people there—women, men, children, and even grandparents in the crowd, and many were not even patients. The boy who told Virgil about Jacques, the miner boy, stood in front of her. She tapped him on the shoulder.

"*J-j-ambo*," he said.

"*Jambo sana*. What's your name?" Therese asked.

"E-E-Eric," he stuttered. He had a jagged scar on his cheek. Poor kid, she thought. The eye above the scar watered, and when he went to brush away the tear, she noticed a woven bracelet on his wrist that looked just like a new one that Virgil had. Maybe they made them and exchanged them as a sign of friendship. Therese asked him what was going on.

It took him what seemed like hours to explain, "The m-miner boy die-died. E-e-everyone w-w-ants to hear what Robert s-says. Amy came in to-to-to-to interview p-p-p-patients. N-n-n-now she's just trying to-to-to . . ." he stammered.

Therese could not stand to listen anymore and murmured, "Thanks."

She stood on her tiptoes to see Robert. Instead of looking sad about his brother, his expression was angry. Dr. Bingi pushed his way through the crowd and stood behind Robert. He placed his giant hands on his shoulders and gave him a strong squeeze.

Therese was surprised the doctor could perform surgeries with those big hands.

"Did your brother see my son?" someone in the crowd yelled in Swahili.

"Did he know my wife?" someone else asked. Suddenly everyone was shouting at once. Amy held Robert's hand. Therese had so many questions of her own but could not bring herself to ask. Dr. Bingi cleared his throat loudly. He spoke Swahili to all the village people who did not understand anything else.

"Let's give Robert the respect he deserves! We have all lost loved ones. He can't tell you anything if you're all yelling."

Robert's French was not very good, but that was the language he used for the cameras. His voice was strong when he said, "I need to go home and tell my aunt and uncle that I'm now the head of my family. My parents are gone, so my younger brothers and sisters need me. I told Amy everything I know, and she promised that she will bring help to those whose family members are still in the mines. Thank God, Free Child Slaves helped me out of the militia group. I am just sorry that they were too late for my brother."

Amy whispered something into his ear, and he looked right at the camera and nodded. The tall gum-chewing cameraman gave Robert a thumbs-up from across the room. Robert looked in Therese's direction and smiled. He repeated the last part of his speech for the camera, more forcefully this time. "Thank God, Free Child Slaves helped me out of the militia. I'm just sad that they were too late to save my brother."

He looked down into his lap and shook his head. Therese could only imagine how hard it must be to know your parents and your brother were dead. The crowd erupted into questions again, and Dr. Bingi helped Robert out of his chair. Amy tried to calm everyone down. Her English got a quick translation from Dr. Bingi.

"Please go back to your morning meal," she said. "I'll call you into the lobby one at a time, if I have news for you!" Her blue eyes twinkled behind her glasses. She tucked her gigantic mass of flaming red hair behind her ears. Although the death of the boy was a tragedy, she looked hopeful and almost happy. The crowd sensed it also and crushed forward to mob her and Robert. Dr. Bingi put a protective arm around her now. The tall, skinny film man followed Robert out the front door. Therese was unsure what to do. To eat breakfast at that point would be impossible, and to wait for Amy could take all day, so she followed Robert and the gum-chomping film man into the yard. It was not easy to catch up with the new celebrity. He moved quickly on his one leg, and the cameraman was tall enough to match his stride.

"Robert!" Therese yelled. He turned, and so did the film man. He pointed his camera at Therese. She rushed up to Robert and threw her arms around him. She almost knocked him off his cane. Suddenly they were both crying. He knew the terrible truth about his brother, while she had hope for hers. He had lost his parents, while she believed her mama was still breathing.

"I'm so sorry," she said lamely.

Robert reached into his pocket and pulled out a slip of paper. It was so dirty, she almost could not read what it said. Through what looked like years-old blood, she read her brother's writing:

I am here. Felix.

Therese's heart jumped. She looked into Robert's eyes and saw the truth. "Jacques had that with him," he whispered. "Your brother is alive." He smiled at her and her face got hot. "The camera's waiting for you," he said. "Use your gift, Therese. Make it count."

She was stunned until she realized the camera was still on her. The gum that the tall, skinny man chewed smelled like watermelon, and her stomach growled. Amy joined him. She held the microphone on a long stick and stepped closer to them. Therese straightened up and switched from Swahili to English. She swallowed spit and looked into the lens.

"You have heard our terrible stories. My village was burned, my father was killed, my mama and little brother were taken away. And I was raped. Robert's brother died yesterday after delivering this note that my brother wrote. My name is Therese, and I am going to find my family. Do not forget me!"

Robert smiled at her through his tears and got into the Free Child Slaves truck. The cameraman, the tall, skinny *mzungu*, focused in on the bloodstained note she showed to him. Therese felt like she held a ticket to something great in her hand. This was her second clue from Felix. It would be her ticket out, and she would find him.

Before Amy left with the cameraman, she asked everyone again to go back to their normal routines. It was impossible. During group discussion, Dr. Bingi tried to keep the meeting in order, but all the kids were chattering excitedly, hoping for news of their families. Therese could not even look at Virgil. Although Virgil was a brave boy, Therese felt he was acting like a coward, hiding away in the hospital. She told that to the group. Dr. Bingi said Therese was not being fair to her unbrother, that he was only ten and not as mature as she. He explained that everyone wasn't ready to leave at the same time. Because Virgil was the priest's son and Felix's best friend, Therese did not want to listen to Dr. Bingi make excuses for Virgil's jump from the play structure in the middle of the night.

Therese kept looking out the window and back down at Felix's note. She wanted to talk to the group about it but could not concentrate. She kept thinking about Robert and his loss and his bravery and his smile. Her daydreaming was interrupted when Amy stepped in. Amy had never interrupted the group meeting before, but that day was special. Dr. Bingi told Therese to go with her.

Therese followed her through the lobby and into an office she had not seen before. It was small, like a closet. Amy gestured for Therese to sit. Amy sat behind a desk, smiled, and sighed. She removed her glasses and pinched where they were resting.

"It's a big day here, Therese," she said in English.

"Yes," Therese said. She was dying at that point. Did Amy have answers for her, or not?

"Last week we went with the UN to your village. Until yesterday, it wasn't safe for us to go back. The militia group had set up camp just behind the houses, on the shore of the lake. As you know, lots of people were killed there, and in the market too. Because you came in with Virgil, you're considered his temporary guardian for now. We understand that he is an only child. Is that right?" Her hair seemed to have grown during the morning. Because Therese had been able to bathe every day, she'd not had to shave her head. It was growing in, and she wondered if she should let it stay wild, like Amy's, or have someone braid it. Amy could tell her mind had wandered, and she pulled out a hair tie to control her flaming curls. Therese snapped back to the conversation about Virgil.

"Yes," Therese said. "His parents tried, but they could not have any more children. They were very old when Virgil was born."

Amy looked down at her lap. "I have sad news about his parents," she said. "They didn't make it, Therese."

Amy reached across to take her hand. Therese felt like a rock had hit her in the chest. Their priest was dead? Virgil's parents were gone? Then he was right. He was an orphan. Therese shook her head. What happened when a village had no priest? Therese asked Amy what would happen to Virgil.

"We're trying to work with the hospital to get him placed with nearby relatives, but we're having a hard time finding his parents' families. With his new injury, he can stay in the hospital in the meantime, but if FCS cannot find his family, the hospital will try to place him in foster care." Amy paused, then continued, "And if that doesn't work, you'll probably become his guardian."

That was too much for Therese to understand. She heard the ticking of a wall clock behind her. It sounded so loud that Therese needed to decide something, and fast. She told Amy that she was only eleven, and not ready to be Virgil's parent.

"I know it's a lot for you to think about, but right now I want to talk to you about that slip of paper Robert gave you." She leaned back in her chair and took a deep breath. Amy's eyes welled up and she said, "We found your father's body. I'm so sorry. I hope there will be a proper ceremony for everyone who lost their lives in the attack."

"Thank you," Therese said through her own tears. She was glad the tall cameraman was not there to see her cry even though she already knew her papa was dead.

"We didn't find your mother or brother among the dead, Therese. We think, like you do, that they're still alive, and probably in the militia group or the mines."

Therese sucked in her breath. Before she could ask anything, Amy told her, "Free Child Slaves is interested in your story. We were profiling Robert, but now that his story's been told, we want to talk to you again."

Therese remembered what Robert told her to say.

"I have a gift. A gift that Mama gave me. I can speak English." She said it like she had something expensive to sell her.

"And this gift is a big one. It's a tremendous opportunity for you. An interview without a translator or subtitles is something we can use. We'll even pay you."

Even though Therese was not sure it was true, she said, "Finding Mama and Felix will be enough payment for me."

"Don't say that," Amy said. "Therese, your story can help you in more ways than one."

When she hugged Amy at the door, Therese felt a kind of love for the woman. Her hair smelled like The City, like The City's cook fires. When Therese was near Desanges, she smelled like flowers because she had been inside the hospital walls and had used a proper shower, but this *mzungu* smelled like the world outside the hospital walls. She smelled like freedom.

—ɯ—

Therese could not sleep. But even though she was up all night, she was not tired. She felt a hope that she had not felt in weeks.

Like Mama and Felix were just outside her door. It had been a strange life in that place between what was and would be. Therese had made friends there, like Odette and Esther. She did not want to leave them, but they, like the hospital staff, knew she could not stay. Therese thought about Virgil. What if his uncles and aunts never came for him? She could not take him with her; his leg was broken, and he was too young for the journey she needed to take to find her own family. She was still puzzling over how to do it when she heard a rooster send up his morning call.

She slipped from her bed and tiptoed past Odette. She looked like a mountain under her sheets, even when she lay on her side. She would be a mother any day now. She was one of the lucky girls there. When she arrived, she started taking computer and language classes, and she might be able to get a job in The City once she and the babies were well enough.

Therese crossed the courtyard. Even Esther was not awake that early. The ground near the play structure was loose dirt, but the rocks that made up the wall around the hospital were volcanic. They, and the dust she walked through, came from a nearby volcano. In her village, they had a breathtaking view of it. On clear nights, Felix and Therese could see the fire at the top of the mountain. Therese realized that she missed The Volcano. She wanted to go back.

She ran her hand against the jagged, volcanic stone. A mosquito found Therese, and it bit her neck. She swatted at it. Another mosquito heard she tasted good and went to work on her ankle. Her whole short life, she had lived in a dangerous place. Safe then behind those stones, she felt restless for the world outside. If she had the strength of The Volcano, she felt she could break the walls.

CHAPTER SIX

~~~~~~~~~

Later, after morning cleanup, Therese returned to her room. Odette perched on her blankets like the Buddha that Therese had seen in a history book. Her belly stuck out over her knees, and she smiled. She held a package out to Therese. She opened the wrapping paper and discovered a blank book with a fabric cover. The cover's colorful pattern reminded Therese of red and orange flowing lava.

"It's for your story," Odette said. "I need to give it to you now. I found out from Dr. Bingi that the babies are ready to be delivered. Who knows how much time I'll have for crafts once they're born?"

After they finished hugging, Therese asked where she'd go.

"I applied to a high school in Paris. If I'm accepted, I can bring my babies. I can go to school, and there's a family that we can live with . . ."

Therese looked surprised, and Odette put her hand on top of Therese's.

"But who will pay for all this? Your food, home, clothing?" asked Therese.

"The Congo Project will help me do all of that," said Odette. Therese looked at her blankly. She had never heard of the Congo Project. She did not know that Odette had a way out.

"You're so lucky, Odette!" Therese whined. She was happy to hear her news but could not imagine the hospital without her.

"It's not luck. It's hard work. If I get out of here with my children, it is because I spent months healing and learning in here. Before I arrived, I couldn't even fill out a high school application. I didn't know how to make a fabric journal . . ."

"But your body was broken. You still have two babies," Therese heard herself say. The conversation was getting more and more complicated. Talking about Odette getting dragged around and damaged by rapists made Therese want to leave the room, but she knew she must stay.

Odette said, "I love my babies. And I want them to get out of this mess. Congo is no place to be a child."

Therese asked her how she could love babies that she did not even know yet. But Therese already had the answer. Mama and Papa often told her that when she was inside Mama's belly, they already loved her.

"I love my children because I love myself, and because they're mine," Odette said simply. Still Therese wondered at the difference between Odette, who loved her babies, and Esther, who seemed not to care about her own.

There was a knock on their door. It was Valentin.

"Dr. Bingi wants to see you for your sonogram, Odette," he said. Therese helped her off the bed and watched her go. She wondered what it would be like, having babies of her own. She looked around her room. Aside from the note from Felix and the second-hand clothes she got at the hospital, the little cloth book was all she could say was truly hers. She sat on her bed and opened the book. In the best English she could remember, she wrote down everything that got her there. She told it like a story, as if she were speaking into the skinny *mzungu*'s camera. She started with: *We need to go, Therese, before the men with the guns find us.*

In the afternoon, Dr. Bingi and Therese had a meeting in the listening center. He called her there to talk about Virgil and about what would await her outside the volcanic rock walls of the hospital. Earlier in the day, he and Amy had met with Virgil to tell him the sad news about his parents. Therese was glad to have not been there for the conversation.

Dr. Bingi told Therese that Virgil understood that he would not go home again. He reminded Therese that Virgil was lucky that he had an injury that would keep him in the hospital for a while, and that the staff was trying to keep him out of the orphanage by locating his aunts and uncles. Therese asked if there was anything she could do to help. Dr. Bingi placed a strong hand on her shoulder and smiled with his eyes.

"The best thing you can do now is to draw attention to your story," he said. "It'll help you find your mama and brother. It will also help the rest of the world recognize the atrocities here. Kids like Virgil have a much better chance of success if people know about them."

Therese asked him where she would go when it was time to leave, and he gave her the news that changed everything. "You will travel with the film crew and Robert to tell your story from the beginning. They'll probably want you to return to your village and to the market. Do you think you can do that?" he asked. She told him yes, as long as the bad men were gone. He understood that she was nervous, and he told her that they would have an escort at all times. Therese thought about the man with the twisty mustache and wondered if he would drive them around. She had so many questions for Dr. Bingi that she did not know where to start. Therese thought about what Odette told her about what happened when girls went back to their villages, but then she remembered that her village was gone. She asked him where she would live. Dr. Bingi shifted in his chair and adjusted his pants, as if they were too tight.

"You can't stay here," he said. "We sometimes send girls in your situation to Brianna's Village." She asked him who Brianna was, and he told her Brianna was a wealthy white woman from the United States who helped build a center near the market where women and girls like Therese could live and be safe until they got back on their feet. "The woman who runs it is a rape survivor named Olivia," Dr. Bingi went on. "She can take care of you. It's not a vacation though. You have to work on her farm in order to stay there. The only way she can afford to take in more boarders is to put them to work. If you find your mama and Felix, it might be a good place for them to stay too."

It was a hard thing to take in. Therese had thought that there must be someone from her village who she could live with, but she could not seem to form the words to ask if there were any other survivors from her town.

"I'm used to farming, and I am not afraid of hard work," she said. The truth was that she did not plan to spend much time at Brianna's Village. She had to find Mama and Felix, and she could not do that if she were planting cassava. But it was closer to home, and it was a roof over her head, so she agreed.

"Okay then. I'll contact Free Child Slaves and Olivia and let them know you're coming. Amy will go with you to introduce you to everyone," he said. Therese thanked him.

Therese went out into the sunlight to find Virgil, and she did not have to look far. He and Stuttering Eric sat on the swings with Odette. Virgil hung his head low and cried. Odette stroked his head and held his hand. Eric listened while holding Virgil's crutches.

"I'm so stupid," Virgil said through his tears. He had finally realized that perhaps he should not have jumped from the play structure.

"I w-w-would have d-d-done the same th-th-th-thing," said Eric, as he pointed to Virgil's cast. Therese walked up and hugged Virgil. She did not know what to tell him. He begged her to take him with her. He tried to convince her he could go fast on his crutches.

"I can't take you with me. All I can do is tell them about you. You're part of my story. I can't tell it without you in it," Therese explained. He stared at her. She told him she would look for his aunts and uncles, but he still stared at her. She did not know what else to do for him, so she looked at the ground. Eric's flip-flops hardly touched the dirt, he was so small. Virgil's one foot rested on the dust, while the bandaged one stuck up a bit. Odette's feet were enormous. They looked like soccer balls with toes. The twins made her feet swell so big that she had to be barefoot all the time. All the feet in the place had run from the bad men and from violence. How much farther would they all run?

"Help me up," said Odette. Therese grabbed her hands and pulled. She grunted as she got to her feet and then kissed Virgil on the head. They walked to their room. Odette held one hand over her belly and the other over her low back. She could hardly walk anymore, so Therese hooked her arm through Odette's.

"Tomorrow's the big day," she said, smiling. Because of her surgery, she would be in the hospital ward for a week. They arrived at their room and packed up some clothes for her, hesitating to zip the bag, as if closing it somehow made it real that she was leaving. Therese wondered how she would feel, living in their room all by herself. She shared one with her parents and brother, and now she was used to sharing with Odette. Therese was nervous about being alone. Odette told her she would be just across the courtyard. That Therese should not worry because she would be back soon. They would not let her lie in that bed for long. She would make such a nice mama, always smoothing people's hair and telling them it would be okay.

Amy returned and met Therese in the tiny closet office. Before they could greet each other, the tall skinny man with the gum and the camera squeezed in too. Amy said, "This is Jeff, my cameraman . . ."

"Are you his boss?" Therese giggled. Jeff laughed and said, "She's my boss because she's my wife!"

Therese's mouth fell open. Amy explained, "We met in America, where I started FCS, and we moved to The City to tell stories of child slaves in order to help get them out of the mines and ranks of the militias."

"We work with the UN to free children and their families in Congo," said Jeff.

Therese wondered what it would be like to live in a place like America. She had a hard time picturing any woman as a man's boss in Congo. Amy must be strong. Therese felt good about telling Amy her story. She and Jeff sat across the table from her. Amy asked if she could say a bit about herself, before the attack, because it was the best place to start.

"My name is Therese," she said. "I am eleven years old. I lived with my family in a village near The City on the shore of a small lake. I have a brother, Felix. He is nine years old. He is my first friend." Amy interrupted her. She asked if she had any other brothers and sisters. Jeff pointed his camera at Therese. She felt as if she should hide, but the camera never shot bullets, so Therese tried to relax. She told Amy her Mama had two other children, one girl before her. She died of typhus when Therese was a baby. Also there was another brother, younger than Felix, but he died of malaria when he was four. His name was Lewis, and he was very sweet, Therese said.

"Mama says this kind of dying is part of life," she explained, clapping her hands and opening them to Heaven. She was aware of this gesture only when she made it in front of the camera. It made her aware of everything, her hands, her feet, her face, her hair. Therese thought about how her hair was starting to grow wild, like Amy's.

"Do you need a rest?" asked Amy. Therese studied Amy's blue eyes behind the glasses. Then she looked at Jeff. She wanted to keep talking. It felt good.

"Tell us about Felix. What is he like?" muttered Jeff, from behind the camera. Therese told him that Felix was very smart. Mama and Papa could afford to send him to school, but only because Papa was a teacher there. Felix and Therese could talk in three languages: Swahili, English, and French. Mama never thought it fair that Felix got to go to school, when Therese couldn't, so she taught Therese how to speak and read. Everything the boys learned at school, Mama had also learned at school in The City, and she taught Therese at home. She explained to Jeff's camera that Felix was very clever.

"He made treasure hunts by writing messages like this, on a slip of paper." She showed the camera the slip of paper that came from Jacques, the miner boy. The camera whizzed a bit, and the glass eye inside changed size. Amy asked what else they should know about Felix. Jeff shifted a little with his camera. Amy held the microphone toward Therese, who slouched in her seat.

"He is a good fisherman, and a good soccer player too. But not as good as Virgil, our friend," she explained, and stared down at her lap. There was a long pause.

"Is it okay to talk about Virgil?" Therese asked.

"Go ahead."

"Virgil and Felix are close in age. We are like a brother and sister to Virgil because he does not have any brothers and sisters of his own." Before she knew it, she was crying. Somehow Therese could not bring herself to say more about Virgil. Amy sighed and looked at Jeff, who shrugged. Amy said she thought it was time for a break. She led Therese into the hallway and put her arm around her shoulder. *The film crew must get tired of kids like me crying,* thought Therese.

"I don't know if I can leave Virgil here," she told Amy.

"You need to let us help you find your family," Amy said. "Virgil will be fine here with Dr. Bingi. The hospital can take better care of him than you can."

Leaving Odette felt okay to Therese because she never knew her before the hospital, and Therese knew Odette would be all right without her. But leaving Virgil felt like leaving Felix. Amy suggested Therese show her and Jeff around the hospital instead of talking about Virgil. She knew they were already familiar with the hospital, and that the tour was for the film they were making about her.

As they walked out into the sunshine, Therese told Jeff he looked too tall for the little office. He laughed and said, "I'm too tall for everything. You should see me in the Jeep!"

First she showed them the lobby and told them it was where she first met Desanges and Valentin. Then they continued to the hallway outside the examination room. Amy told Jeff that he could not shoot any of the women inside because it was their own private business if they were getting examined. Valentin stepped out of a room and into the hall.

"This is Valentin," Therese said. He flexed his big muscles under his militia tattoo, hugged her, and waved to the camera. They continued outside, and as always Virgil was hanging around with Stuttering Eric. He balanced on his crutches and kicked a soccer ball to Eric with his good foot. Therese pointed to Virgil.

"This is Virgil. He saved my life in the cassava field. He is my unbrother, and he broke his leg . . ."

"*Jambo sana!*" interrupted Virgil. They watched him try to kick the ball again, but he was pretty slow on the crutches. They continued on to Therese's room. Jeff cursed as he hit his tall head on the doorframe. He gasped and coughed as he swallowed his gum. Odette giggled at him as she made up her bed, for the last time. Her side of the room did not have donated clothes in it anymore. They had all been packed for her stay in maternity. Therese introduced the camera to her and put her hand over Odette's belly. Odette hid her smile with her hand.

"And who's that?" asked Amy, gesturing to the big belly. Therese translated for her.

"My twins," said Odette in Swahili, and Therese interpreted.

"They will join us tomorrow. You should come back for that," Therese said jokingly. The crew had a long day, so they finished with the girls' joking about the babies.

Amy told Therese that Olivia had a place for her at Brianna's Village and was expecting her soon, but Therese wanted to see Odette's babies first.

Therese and Odette spent the night talking about what would come next. Who knew what would happen to them? These were their mysteries. Therese asked her how she felt about leaving the hospital someday. Odette said that only God knew what would happen once she reached Paris.

"Virgil and I came here together, but we'll leave separately," Therese said. "At least you get to leave with your family, even if they're only babies." Odette clapped once in the dark, and Therese knew she was opening her hands toward Heaven, the way Therese did, as if to say, "That is the truth."

—⁓—

The next morning, the girls were sleepy from talking all night. Therese carried Odette's bag to the maternity ward. Odette looked happy to be getting rid of her giant belly. Therese could not believe how straight she could stand up, even with two babies inside. Desanges met them at the door. She smelled delicious, like soap and roses. She asked Odette if she was ready. Therese's friend nodded and turned to face her. Therese gave her a big hug and wished her luck. Valentin arrived with a wheelchair and took Odette down the hall to become a mother. Desanges patted Therese's shoulder.

"They're so much easier to take care of on the inside," she said, but Therese did not know if she was talking about babies, or girls in the hospital. Therese headed back to her room, intending to write in the book that Odette made for her. She was surprised to find Virgil sitting on her front porch. He held out a full breakfast plate to her. She sat and took it from him, wondering how he got it all the way there from the kitchen. He said Therese needed to eat. She could not believe that little Virgil was telling her that. He said she'd need it for her trip. Therese asked him what he meant, and he told her that her papers went through, and she was leaving

that day. Stuttering Eric told him. Eric managed to know all about
everything that went on in the hospital. Therese was comforted
that Virgil had Eric to keep him company. He pulled out a woven
bracelet from his pocket and handed it to her. It was like the ones
he and Eric wore, but hers was red instead of brown. She told him
that she didn't have anything for him.

"Write about me. Tell my story. That'll be for me," he said. She
wondered if Dr. Bingi told him to say that, but she did not care.
She reached over and took his hand.

"You are my best unbrother," she said.

He struggled onto his crutches and started to tripod away.

"I am your only unbrother!" he said jokingly over his shoulder.
She ate the breakfast he had brought—cassava, pineapple, beans,
eggs—and thought about how, without him, she could still be running hungry through the bush. Or worse.

Desanges found Therese to tell her Odette's twins had been
born. A girl named Sara and a boy named Noah. Dr. Bingi was
busy sewing up her friend and cleaning up her babies. She was
happy to hear about the birth of Odette's children, but then Valentin ran up and led her to the main building, announcing that
Therese was the guest of honor, and she realized that there was a
party in the cafeteria, just for her, to celebrate her departure.

All her friends in the hospital were there. She saw Esther and
her owl-eyed baby, Desanges, Stuttering Eric, Virgil, and Valentin.
Even Amy was there with Jeff. It was a party, and everyone was
singing, so she joined in.

> *Celebrate our sister*
> *A new day has begun for her*
> *Celebrate our sister*
> *She is so strong*

Amy and Therese went to her room to pack her things. Into
Therese's plastic bag she put the secondhand clothes given to her

by the hospital, the notes from Felix, her journal, and the bracelet Virgil made for her. Amy pulled the sheets and blanket from her bed and threw them into a hamper near the door. They stepped outside and crossed the courtyard. There was one last thing she needed to do. Therese needed to see Odette's babies.

Amy walked with her into maternity. Desanges sat at the front desk and sipped the last of her passion fruit juice. She stood, grinning, and walked them to Odette's room. Her friend lay, propped up by pillows, looking relieved. In the crook of one arm was Noah. He had light skin and flat cheekbones. Therese could not believe how tiny he was. At her breast was Sara. She was much bigger than her twin, dark as the night, with a big, round face, just like Odette's. The babies did not look as if they came from the same mother, but to tell her this would only remind her of how they got inside her. Instead Therese told her she was a beautiful mama. Odette smiled at Therese and whispered that this was where her life really began.

Amy reminded her that Jeff was waiting in the Jeep and that they had to go. Therese asked her how Odette and she would stay in touch.

"I'll be here visiting Virgil," Amy explained. "I can deliver letters for you." Odette nodded. Therese gave her a big hug and kissed both babies. It was confusing for Therese, leaving her like that, but she knew Odette would be going someplace else soon. Before Therese cried, she allowed Amy to lead her out. They passed the courtyard, where the boys playing soccer took advantage of Virgil's crutches. He was playing goalie. Therese could not bring herself to hug him goodbye. They waved at each other as the other team scored. Amy and Therese walked through the lobby and out into the hot sunlight.

CHAPTER SEVEN

The drive to Brianna's Village took more than an hour. Their driver, Thomas, was a fat Rwandan who acted as the FCS translator when Jeff and Amy were in the field. He sweated so much that he needed to turn on the air conditioning. The truck was freezing. Therese looked out the window and noticed that the potholes of The City had given way to a smooth highway. Huge mountains rose in the distance, and the air was clear. Healthy-looking cane sprouted in the foreground. If there were not so many bad men, it might be a nice place to go on a vacation. But there were bad men, forcing boys to do bad things for them. Therese's mind wandered. She pictured Robert's lips.

"When will we see Robert again?" Therese asked.

Amy said, "Robert's busy telling his family about Jacques. They need some time together. We'll meet up with him later in the week." Therese was a little disappointed. She needed to see him again and thank him for all he did to help her. Mostly she just wanted to see his beautiful smile.

—⁓—

Every now and then, they passed a UN truck or another *mzungu* vehicle, but out there on the highway, they were pretty much the only ones around. They drove through a little village, where two women bathed in a river with their children. They pointed at the

FCS truck and called out. The truck passed through some thick woods. The bright sun gave way to near darkness, as if the sun had been turned off. Then they emerged back into the sun, shocking Therese as she looked out the window at lush, green cassava fields. On the other side of the crops was a dusty little compound with a long, wood-shingled house, a large lean-to with chairs underneath, a cooking area, and a wooden outbuilding. Thomas slowed down.

"This is Brianna's Village," said Amy.

Jeff focused his lens on Therese and asked what she thought.

"I thought it would be bigger," said Therese. "This does not look like a village. Where is the market? Where is the church?"

Amy said, "It's a place to stay safe. It will be fine, Therese. Remember that it's only temporary, until we find your family."

Children ran out and gathered around the truck. They stuck their hands into the windows, begging for a treat or some money. Several of their mamas also gathered around and swatted their hands away. The kids backed off, as a short, serious woman with round cheeks walked up. She nodded at the truck, and Amy and Jeff jumped out. Thomas struggled from the driver's seat. Therese stepped out into the hot, bright sun. She squinted into the eyes of the round-cheeked woman.

"I am Olivia," she said. She kissed Therese's left, right, and left cheeks. As she leaned in, Therese noticed a large scar under Olivia's ear. It snaked down her neck, to her chest, and into her *kanga*. Therese wondered how she got it.

"Can I film?" asked Jeff. Thomas, fist-bumping a small boy, translated for him.

"Yes, but do not film that girl," Olivia said, pointing at a scared-looking girl with a black eye and a split lip. "Her husband tried to kill her last week and is still looking for her." The girl looked so young that Therese could not believe she was married. Therese looked around and realized that there were no men on the compound, aside from Thomas and Jeff. There were boys, but no men.

"Can you show us around?" asked Amy. Olivia nodded. She waved off the women and children and took them on a tour of

Brianna's Village. It was much bigger than it looked from the highway. Several buildings veered off behind the main house. They followed Olivia down a long dirt passageway, ducking to avoid some clothes hanging from a line strung between buildings. She led them to the back of her home and opened the door. Therese was surprised to see not only a wooden floor, but also wooden-paneled walls. There were several wooden chairs and couches with cozy-looking cushions on them.

"I built this all with my own two hands," Olivia proudly explained. "I wanted this to be a comfortable place for the women and children."

"Maybe this won't be so bad," thought Therese. She was impressed with its uncluttered simplicity.

Olivia walked them down a hallway to a bedroom. It was small but inviting, with a colorful fabric covering the window. Two mattresses lay on the floor. On one of the beds slept two naked babies facedown. It must have been naptime. They followed her to the next room. It was identical to the first, but instead of babies on the bed, there were pillows and blankets and clean *kangas*. In a corner was a large suitcase with a padlock on the zipper.

Olivia said, "This is a typical bedroom. It's mine." It made Therese feel good that her bedroom was the same as everyone else's.

She led them outside to the cooking area. A cook stove and a large pile of charcoal waited for someone to come and make dinner. On an outdoor shelf were utensils and bowls and pots. Many chairs were stacked in a corner.

"Thirty-two people live here and about half are children," she explained. Olivia walked them to the lean-to. It was covered by plastic tarps and had many folding chairs and benches inside. There was only a dirt floor there, and a single bulb hung from an extension cord in the middle of the tepee-style ceiling. "This is the sharing center. We all fit in here for morning meeting. It's where many decisions are made."

Therese did not really know what she meant, but she was sure she would find out. Her eyes followed the extension cord from the top of the lean-to, over the house and off to she-did-not-know-where. The generator maybe. Olivia watched her eyes and said, "It goes to the outhouse."

At the hospital, Therese became used to using western-style bathrooms and running water. Electricity and plumbing were not things they wanted for in the hospital. Still the village was more like her own home. She noticed a pile of jerry cans behind the sharing center. Therese knew she'd be asked to draw water from the river, and she did not mind. Olivia's cell phone rang. It made Therese jump, hearing a ringing telephone way out there in the countryside. She walked a little distance away.

Amy asked Therese, "Do you think you're ready to spend some time here?"

"I think so," she replied. "I have many questions though." She had forgotten that Jeff's camera was still recording. He aimed it all around the compound and settled on a little toddler in a yellow dress. She dropped her bottle of formula and frowned at him. She had probably never seen such a tall, white person. Therese picked up her bottle, wiped off the nipple, and handed it to her. She had little dimples and smiled at Therese.

"What do you want to ask?" Amy said.

"How long will I be here? What kind of work will I do? Where do I sleep? When will I be able to find my brother and mama?" she began, but could not end, as there were so many questions.

"You'll be here as long as it takes," said Olivia, walking up behind them. She surprised Therese by answering her in French. "Your jobs change daily. You'll cook, clean, farm, draw water, and mend clothes. It'll be hard work, but if you do it well, I'll teach you some skills that can help you when you leave. You'll share a room with me until you're ready to share with another girl. Did I answer your questions?"

"Yes. Except the one about my family."

"That I can't answer. Only God knows," Olivia said. She clapped her hands once and opened them skyward. Therese liked her already.

Dusk was approaching. Therese looked around and saw that the crowd had appeared again. Without any prompting, chairs were brought out, cook fires started, and children brought out jerry cans of water. Somebody started singing a syncopated chant. It was one Therese recognized from church, and it reminded her that before she arrived, she came from someplace else. Amy was being eaten by mosquitoes and swatted at them.

"We're losing light," she said to Olivia. "We'll be back in the morning." Thomas translated for Olivia, but Therese had a feeling she did not need it.

"Of course," Olivia said. "I'll get Therese moved in right now."

"If you need me, you can call anytime," Amy said. "Olivia knows my number." She gave Therese a big hug and handed her the plastic bag. Therese waved at Amy, Jeff, and Thomas as they got into the truck. When they drove down the dusty hill and back onto the highway, Therese was a little nervous. It was the first time she had spent the night alone among strangers. Even at the hospital, Virgil was with her. Therese closed her eyes and tried to hold back tears. Olivia put her arms around Therese.

"Everybody cries the first night," she said, consoling her. "But then you need to get over it." Therese heard the familiar singing and chanting and wanted to go home.

—⁓—

The next morning, Therese helped to draw water from the river. Nobody seemed to worry about bad men on the road, so she walked across the highway to the water with some girls who were about her age. One, named Mwamini, was friendly. She was the mother of Giselle, the little girl in the yellow dress. As they walked back and forth with jerry cans on their heads, they got to know each other. Therese was surprised that Mwamini was sixteen and had a husband. Yet she was at Brianna's Village. Almost every girl Therese met at the hospital was a young mama without a husband. Mwamini was married at fourteen, and she and her husband had Giselle, but when the bad men came and raped her, Mwamini had to leave home. She carried a bad man's baby, a boy, until her husband cut it from her belly. She almost died from her husband's attack, but Olivia found her in the bush, took her to the hospital, and had cared for her since. She said that she was looking for a sponsor, someone to get her out of Congo. When Therese told her about the film Free Child Slaves was making about her, Mwamini became a little jealous and stopped listening. Therese quickly realized that she needed to be more careful about who she told her story to. Not everyone was as lucky as she.

By the time breakfast was served, her story had spread like lice. Mwamini told all the girls about the film. Instead of feeling proud, Therese was embarrassed. She heard the word "famous" and "celebrity" when she walked by. Giselle toddled up to Therese and offered her bottle and dimples to go with it. Mwamini snatched Giselle away. Therese was the enemy, it seemed. She would need to keep her mouth shut, but Therese did not know if that would be enough now.

When it was time to eat, Therese sat alone. Giselle screamed from her mama's lap, wanting to get down and join her. Therese smiled at her from her chair, but Mwamini did not let her down. Olivia took Mwamini aside during the meal. Mwamini put Giselle down to speak with Olivia. The toddler came over and ate from Therese's plate while her mother frowned at them. A few moments later, Olivia brought Mwamini to talk with Therese.

"I'm sorry I treated you badly," she said when Olivia poked her. Therese did not know what to say, so she stared at Giselle.

"We are a community here," Olivia said. "We're sisters in survival."

"I'm sorry, my sister," said Mwamini. It was a strange thing to say. Only Felix called her his sister. Mwamini held out her hand and Therese took it. Olivia smiled and said, "Well done."

Inside the sharing center was very hot. The gravel made for a poor surface for the toddlers who sat at their mothers' feet. Unlike at breakfast, suddenly everyone wanted to sit near Therese. She knew it was because the film crew was coming. Mwamini squeezed in next to her.

As Olivia walked in, Therese saw most of the boys, dressed in school uniforms, lined up along the highway. An armed guard appeared and led them on foot, off to school. Just like in Therese's village, only boys were allowed to learn. Giselle sat at her mama's feet and banged a bottle-top with a rock. It seemed to amuse her.

"*Jambo*," said Olivia.

"*Jambo sana*," said the group.

"We have a new sister. Please welcome Therese," she commanded.

"Welcome," said the sisterhood.

"We have no secrets here. We are all equal. As part of our hospitality, Therese, we feed you, clothe you, and give you a safe place to sleep, share with you, and help you get back on your feet. Your job is to share with us, work with us, and help this village continue to be a safe place for women and children. I think there's been enough gossip going around here already." Therese noticed Olivia's sharper tone, as she looked meaningfully at Mwamini and then back at Therese. "Why don't you tell us how you got here?"

Therese felt she had told this story a thousand times, but she knew that telling it again would help her tell it better the next time. As she finished, she heard murmuring near the back of the tent. She could hear the approaching truck. One of the little girls outside ran to meet it.

"Before the film crew gets here, does anyone have any questions?" asked Olivia. The girl with the split lip and black eyes cleared her throat.

"I am Hiroute," she said meekly. Therese noticed that many of her teeth were missing near the cut in her lip. Hiroute could not meet Therese's eyes.

"*Jambo*," Therese said.

"I'm new here too. I can show you the farm, if you like," she offered.

"That's generous of you, Hiroute, but Mwamini will do it," said Olivia. "Do you have something else to share?"

Hiroute said, "After the bad men tortured me, I returned to my husband and his family, but they wouldn't take me back unless I brought money. I turned to prostitution. When I returned to my husband, I had money, but I was also ill with HIV, and he tried to kill me. I'm here because Olivia will teach me to survive on my own."

Therese thought about how she'd been wearing her favorite Sunday dress when the man hit her with his gun and hurt her. Wondering if Hiroute was taking the same kinds of medicine she had to take to stay healthy, Therese looked around the sharing center. How many of these girls were on medications because of the bad men? How many of them had HIV?

Therese wondered if Hiroute rehearsed her story, the way Therese rehearsed hers, over and over again. She felt sorry that Hiroute did not have a film crew of her own.

"Thank you for sharing," said Olivia. The film crew had slipped in as quietly as they could, and Jeff sat on the gravel. He was still almost as tall as the rest of the girls and women sitting in chairs. He chomped his gum and waved at everyone. Therese smelled that the day's flavor was mint. Baby Giselle pulled at Jeff's sneaker laces. Amy crouched near him, then stood, hunched over, by the opening in the lean-to. It was getting crowded. Jeff took off his shoe and handed it to Giselle, who began filling it with gravel. Thank goodness she could entertain herself. Mwamini was focused on getting the film crew's attention. She kept smiling at Amy and Jeff. Olivia watched this play out with a furrowed brow. It was already too hot in the tent. Therese felt sweaty.

"We need to tend our fields. If you'd like to join us, we should go outside," Olivia said to Amy and Jeff in French. Mercifully, someone opened the tarp flap. Bright sunlight, fresh air, and children's faces met Therese's.

Amy asked her, "How did your first night go?"

Therese said, "I made a friend" and pointed to Giselle, who toddled over and handed her the sneaker filled with gravel. Jeff laughed.

"Do you want to talk to the camera?" Amy asked Therese.

"Sure. What language?"

"English, please," she said. Therese emptied the shoe and handed it back to Jeff. Amy pulled her red hair into a large knot on her head. *It is going to get very hot,* Therese thought. Amy was smart to put her enormous hair away. She slung a large microphone on her shoulder. Olivia led the whole band to an armed guard. Therese was nervous around men with guns, but Olivia kissed him on both cheeks, like family. He smiled broadly, and Therese could tell he was on their team. He must be why nobody there was afraid of walking on the road alone or drawing water at the river.

"This is Kisungu. He'll walk with you the rest of the way," said Olivia. She turned back toward the compound. Jeff followed them with his camera. Mwamini appeared right next to Therese as they crossed the river. Someone had built a small bridge, and a path led them around a bend. Therese saw a large cassava field and a smaller cane field. There was a shed with tools nearby, and a cat lounged in its shade.

"That's Couchou," said Kisungu, pointing at the cat. She slunk up to Kisungu and wove between his legs. He stroked her between the ears and made kissing noises.

"I can see she is very afraid of his gun," Therese said to the camera. Amy laughed. Jeff gave a thumbs-up. The group went to the shed. Mwamini handed out tools to the women and older children. Several of the girls went to the cane field with machetes. Most of the women brought hoes to the cassava field. Therese looked around and spotted cassava drying in the sun on large blankets. Mwamini pointed to some baskets.

"We need to take the dried cassava back across the highway," Mwamini told the camera. Therese translated for her. Mwamini put a large basket in Therese's hands.

They were the only ones doing this job, and there was enough cassava drying there to keep them busy until dinner. Therese hiked up her *kanga* and stooped to fill her basket. She watched Mwamini only fill hers halfway and wondered why. Was she that lazy? She hoisted hers onto her head and took off across the highway. Therese filled hers all the way, as Mwamini returned with her basket empty. When Therese went to put the load on her head, it was too heavy to lift. She had to dump out half of it to even make it budge. Mwamini started on her second load and laughed at her. Therese looked at the camera and said, "I hate her."

After filming them, Amy and Jeff left to talk to Olivia. Therese thought her job bored them. It bored her, too, but it was so familiar that she welcomed it. She listened to the women in the field sing and she hummed along with them. She could even ignore Mwamini, who continued to tease her about how full her baskets were. The morning passed quickly. It felt good to work again. It felt like home.

Later that afternoon, Amy stopped to talk with her. She looked cheerful, as always, but was badly sunburned. Rivulets of sweat trailed down her neck. Her blue eyes looked even bluer. She wanted to film Therese somewhere else.

"Olivia doesn't want you to come with us today. She says she needs you in the field. But don't worry. We told her that any publicity you get will mean money coming in for her. It's very complicated," she said with a sigh. Therese suggested that maybe Olivia could tell her story to the camera.

"Olivia has told her story. It's not new. Besides, Free Child Slaves can't use it because nobody in her family is in the militias or in the mines," she explained.

"Are they already free?" Therese asked.

"Her daughters are all here," Amy explained. That was confusing. If Olivia's daughters were with her, where were her husband

and sons? Amy said they did not make it. Like Therese's mama, Olivia was a widow. She could not bring herself to ask what happened to Olivia's sons. Therese was too scared, as she did not know what was happening to her own brother. Amy looked at her feet. Jeff approached, hot and tired, like a tall stalk wilting in the heat. Therese stretched her back.

Thomas started the truck's motor, and Therese jumped in beside Amy in the way-back of the SUV. The seats they pulled down looked like a lot of fun, but Therese learned very quickly that they were not. It was bumpy in the way-back, and they nearly fell out of their seats when Thomas took a turn too fast. Amy faced her.

"Therese, we think that in order for us to follow you properly on your journey, we might need you to take us through your village and show us around. Do you think you can do that?" she asked.

"I think so. How bad is it?" Therese asked Amy. She closed her eyes and shook her head.

She told Therese the huts were almost completely burned down. There was a large grave, but the bodies had been removed for identification. Amy said, "You won't see anybody there, if that's what you mean."

"I do not know if I can do it," Therese said. Amy took her hand.

"Can you maybe take us to the market, or to the lake?" Jeff asked. Therese could not answer him. Her tongue seemed stuck to the roof of her mouth.

Amy said, "You understand we want to film you because we think your story will have a happy ending, right?" Therese knew she was just trying to get her to agree to take her to the village. Jeff pulled out his camera. He pointed it out the window at The Volcano. He must have thought it was as stunning as Therese did. She saw smoke rising from the opening of The Volcano. It must have been active in the last few days. She was sorry she missed it. Amy pulled open a small plastic bag. She fished out some crackers and a banana for her. Therese smiled at Amy.

"Okay," Therese said. "I will take you to my home."

CHAPTER EIGHT

O n the way to Therese's village, they passed Papa's school, which was located in the church on the Long Road. Therese strained to find him in the foreground though she knew he would not appear. She would not see Virgil's papa either. Suddenly she did see someone.

"Stop the car!" she yelled.

Thomas slammed on the brakes. Therese saw a small figure in the cane field. It looked like a child, but she knew immediately who it was. She jumped from the FCS truck and ran through the dust churned up from its wheels. Jeff unfolded himself from the back seat and followed her at a sprint.

"Mr. Muhangi! Mr. Muhangi!" she yelled. The old man looked around for her voice. He could hardly see because he was so old. He put his shriveled hand to his brow and squinted toward her. Therese's feet pounded the high grass, and the long stalks whipped her thighs.

"It's me! Therese!" Therese screamed. He grinned at her through the bright sunlight and clapped his hand over his heart. She ran and ran toward him. Jeff tried to keep up with her. She heard him huffing behind her, but she did not stop. Finally Therese had found another survivor from her village! She threw her arms around him, and he gave her a huge hug. He was so happy, he started to weep. She could not bring herself to weep because she was smiling so much.

"God is good! God is good!" he said. She allowed him to hold her for a long time, rocking her back and forth as though she were a baby. She made mewling sounds in his frail arms. Therese thought that the world could not be so cruel a place that it would take away everyone Virgil and she loved. It had not. Mr. Muhangi was alive.

—⁘—

"Mr. Muhangi was one of Papa's best friends," Therese said from the warm embrace. "When Papa was a boy, Mr. Muhangi was his teacher. When he got too old to teach, Mr. Muhangi helped at the school, cleaning up the church and fixing school uniforms." Mr. Muhangi smiled at Therese and patted her head, as Therese continued, "Everyone in my village knew him. He joined us for supper, and he said that it was Mama's cooking that kept him alive. Because his wife died before him, Mama watched out for him."

She gazed at him lovingly.

"This is my friend!" Therese said in Swahili, once he had released her from his big hug. Therese turned to Jeff and remembered her English. "This is Mr. Muhangi!"

She explained to her friend why these *mzungu* people were with her. She introduced him to Thomas, Amy, and Jeff. Thomas was so fat that the run had taken his air away. He was still panting with his hands on his knees and could barely wave at Mr. Muhangi. The old man noticed the camera that Jeff carried. He looked curious and maybe a little nervous.

"Therese, will you ask Mr. Muhangi if he is interested in talking on camera about the village?" asked Amy. She did, and the old man looked more nervous than ever.

"It's just a camera. Not a gun," Thomas said in Swahili, still panting.

Mr. Muhangi was not convinced. "If the bad men see me on television, how do I know they won't come back to kill me too?" he asked. *He is no fool,* thought Therese. She translated for the *mzungu*.

Jeff sighed and chomped his gum. Therese could not believe he didn't choke on it during his run.

"This film isn't for television; it's to educate people in the rest of the world about what is happening to the Congolese people," Jeff explained. "It's for the governments of foreign countries, to put pressure on them to send aid to the DRC." She translated the words, but could not understand everything she translated, and Mr. Muhangi shook his head like he did not believe her. Mr. Muhangi said, "Foreign countries did this. If they didn't want the methane gas in our lake, they wouldn't have hired bad men to kill us for it. This is the history of Congo. Colonists and foreign countries take natural resources out of Africa, enslave locals, and use native thugs like The General to do so."

There was a moment of silence and then Amy interrupted by asking with a smile, "Would anyone like some water?" and without an answer, she stalked through tall grass to the car. Thomas followed her, huffing and puffing all the way. Mr. Muhangi turned to Jeff. He squinted at Jeff's chomping and asked Therese what was wrong with the tall man's mouth. Therese told him the tall man was nervous around smart people like him, and chewing gum calmed him down.

"I don't trust anyone I don't know, after what happened here," Mr. Muhangi told Jeff. "I'll give you my story, but only if it is Therese that aims that gun at me. I'll give Therese my story because it's the only thing I have left to give her." He put an arm around her. Therese translated for Jeff, who nodded to Mr. Muhangi.

Jeff handed her the heavy camera. She'd been very nervous about this, the day she would have to come back to the village. The day she would have to see where Papa was killed. Where Felix and Mama were taken. Where she was attacked. Jeff said, "Sometimes it's easier to see something difficult through the lens of a camera," but she was still nervous. He explained that the camera would help to put distance between her and the subject. All she could promise was that she would try.

Mr. Muhangi smiled as Amy and Thomas returned. Amy carried her big plastic bag of snacks and water. She handed a bottle to Mr. Muhangi and showed him the cookies in the bag. He took a couple and Therese did too. He seemed more ready to answer Amy's questions, now that he had food. He asked if she wanted to know how he survived. He pointed to the high grasses ahead. There were tall cattails growing in the water. Through the stalks, she could see the outline of the red rowboat that they all used at fishing time.

"Mr. Muhangi escaped in that," she said. Amy looked at Mr. Muhangi like she was measuring him. She observed that it seemed like a long way for him to paddle from the other side of the lake, where their village stood. Therese translated for her. Mr. Muhangi gave a hoarse laugh that sounded like ripping paper.

"I've been paddling across this lake in that boat my whole life," he said. "The soldiers' visit just made me paddle faster." He looked toward the camera for a moment, and then looked back at the boat.

"Can we go to the village, so you can both tell your stories on camera?" asked Amy. Therese looked across the lake. A few walls still stood. She squinted into the late day sun, and her brain thought it saw the rest of the village, but her eyes told her there were scorch marks where buildings used to be. She tried to picture herself back home but all the bad things that the bad men did got in the way. Then she thought about Felix, working as a slave in a mine. Then she imagined Mama being dragged around by the soldiers and being raped as Odette was. Then Therese thought about the soldier who attacked her, and Therese told Amy, "I am ready."

Thomas turned back toward the path. He was probably anxious to be back in his car. Mr. Muhangi was probably anxious to be back in his boat. Therese was too. She already knew that Amy and Jeff would never let her go alone in the boat with him. She asked if they could all go in the boat together. Jeff seemed ready to go and shrugged his tall shoulders.

"There's no way I'm getting in that thing," Amy said, laughing. "That boat is tiny, and who knows what lives in the lake." Jeff looked irritated. Therese helped her friend pull the rowboat into the water and settled in next to him. She watched the drama play out.

"Thomas and I can meet you there in the car," Amy told Jeff.

"It's your job as director to be here with us, because we're your crew," Jeff responded. Amy shook her head. Therese looked at her feet. Mr. Muhangi's boat was the same as it always was. The red paint peeled off the side. The inside was dry as a bone.

"If you can take on The General, you can do this," Jeff said. Therese reached for Amy's big microphone, but Amy surprised her by getting in.

"We'll watch out for crocodiles," said Mr. Muhangi. Therese did not translate for him. She moved the paddles out of the way for the crew, but Jeff's great height almost capsized them. Once they were steady, Therese noticed that the afternoon was beautiful. It was a perfect day for fishing. Mr. Muhangi pushed off from shore, and they were on their way.

Back at Brianna's Village, Therese had told Amy she was afraid of what she might see at their village. When she took the camera, she remembered what Jeff had said about it being easier to see something difficult through a lens. It felt good on Therese's shoulder, even if she was still sore from carrying cassava across the highway. Therese shot Jeff and Mr. Muhangi paddling. She barely had to move the camera to pan around the boat.

"Mama used to tell me there was a giant fish at the bottom of the lake," Therese started to say. Mr. Muhangi chimed in that there was no giant fish. Only a giant lie. Therese translated for her *mzungu* friends. The conversation went on like that the whole way across the lake, with Therese saying something, and Mr. Muhangi interrupting her. She told the story about how Felix once used a basketball net he found to catch fish. Mr. Muhangi interrupted and said Virgil was always the best fisherman. It felt just like it used to, only Felix and Virgil were not paddling, and they were not returning home for dinner. As they neared the village, Therese saw vultures circling near the water's edge. It looked like they were fighting over a recent kill. She focused closer on the scene. One of the birds dragged a big, white bone from the water. Sometimes that happened. A wild pig or goat fell into the water, the crocodiles ate it, and once it washed up on the shore, the vultures picked it clean.

She was surprised when Mr. Muhangi jumped from the boat into the shallow water and chased off the birds. She focused the camera in closer and could tell that it was no goat. It was a human arm. The fingers were still attached. Usually something like that would cause Therese to cry and look away, but she found herself zooming in closer. She wanted to share the story with the rest of the world.

"You okay, Therese?" asked Jeff, grabbing the dropped paddle from Mr. Muhangi's side of the boat.

"Yes," Therese gasped. She panned from the scene of Mr. Muhangi swatting away the vultures and up toward the big, dark hills in the background. She did not even feel sad. She had a job to do, and that felt good. She heard Thomas driving up the road to the village. He pulled up and parked the FCS truck near the center of town. Amy reached over and shut off the camera and said, "Cut."

Once they were on solid ground, Mr. Muhangi explained that many of the villagers ran into the lake when the bad men came. Others ran to the hills. Therese did not know if that was true because Virgil and she spent all night up on that hill and did not see anyone. It was strange to stand where they were. It had been the pier where people brought their fish in and it was gone. Also gone was the small marina where they used to tie up their boat. Only the poured concrete from under the marina remained. Jeff offered to take the camera from her, but she wanted to be the cameraperson now. Somehow shooting the scene made her feel less as though a bad thing happened to her, and more as if a bad thing happened to someone else.

"We should probably see what you shot already, just to make sure," Jeff told her. He took the camera from Therese and pushed a button. He swiveled a little television screen around to Mr. Muhangi and her. There, like magic, was the moving image she'd made. She gasped, and so did her friend. There he was, shooing away the vultures! They both laughed, and Amy put her arm around Therese.

Jeff handed the camera back to her. He took the boom microphone from Amy and followed her and Mr. Muhangi, who showed them around. He started with the first house and said, "This used to be the home of the Eglis family."

The only thing left of their home was the tin roof. It was stained black from smoke and fire. He took them through town, or what used to be town. A light wind blew dust through the street. She did not remember the wind. Maybe the buildings that once stood there gave shelter from the moving air. They continued walking. A chicken pecked at the ground. It was much quieter than she remembered, as if only ghosts lived there. Mr. Muhangi took them to the one remaining building. Three walls still stood, and there was burned furniture inside. The Ushindis used to live there. Therese played with their daughters. She asked her friend what happened to them, and he said only that they were gone. She translated for Jeff. Her heart started to hammer in her chest because she knew the next house behind the big tree in the middle of town was hers. She panned the camera up and gazed at the leaves above her. It seemed that the tree was the only whole thing left.

"This was my home," she choked out. Therese panned the camera to where Papa, Mama, Felix, and she scratched their names in the tree years ago. The wind picked up and swirled some papers around their feet. Without looking at them, she knew that they were pages of books. Amy picked one up. There was a flash of recognition on her face.

"Is this *Jane Eyre*?" she asked, showing it to Jeff. Everyone stared at her.

"It was mine," Therese told them. She kept rolling. She felt angry, as Robert did when he spoke before the camera in the hospital's lobby. The concrete foundation was still there, and so was the roof, but barely attached to the one remaining wall. Everything was gone from inside, including the special mixing bowl that was Mama's, the machete that was Papa's, the bed they all shared, and all their books. Therese did not have any more tears now. She was protected behind her camera and was mad. It was a good feeling, to not be sad for a minute.

"My home was over there," said Mr. Muhangi. He led them to where his hut used to be. He had no real foundation. All that was left was a burn mark. He walked on past it, as if it were never there. He sighed. "My house was just a thing, and it's gone now, but it was not important." He turned his back on the camera.

"Where do you live now?" asked Jeff. Therese translated for him.

"At the schoolhouse on the Long Road. It's in the Protestant church and it's the only real thing still standing. I can take you there, but I think you'll want to see this first."

He led them to a large hole in the ground, back in the woods. There were crushed bushes and fallen branches where someone had driven a large truck through the woods. Tire tracks went off in the direction of the road. Therese scrambled down into the hole and shot toward him, as he looked down at her.

"This is where they buried our village. Forty-four people in this hole. The authorities came back to dig them up a few weeks ago. I believe you were here," he said, pointing at Amy. She nodded. She and Jeff helped Therese out of the hole. It was hard to believe that forty-four people could fit in there. Then she remembered Papa, and how they cut him up. That is how they fit all those people. The cookies she'd eaten did not sit so well in her stomach, and suddenly Therese fought the need to throw up. Mr. Muhangi started to sob. She did not know what to do, so she just let the camera roll on him. He walked in the direction of the cassava fields. Therese felt a slow, creeping feeling go up her back, like a big spider was climbing on her. She followed him to where the bad thing happened to Papa and to her. She tried not to think about what she was putting on the camera. She could not talk, so she let Mr. Muhangi do it all for her.

"Many young girls and boys were violated here. Most of the men were murdered. They took some of the young boys away," he said. Jeff asked how many people were in the village before the attack. Therese translated, but they both answered at the same time, her friend in Swahili, and she in English.

"Sixty-seven," they told him. So, not including Therese, Virgil, and Mr. Muhangi, there are twenty others who could still be out there alive. Where were they? Mr. Muhangi shook his head. He said, "The lake is dangerous at night. So is the forest. God willing, they made it to another village nearby. Or the hospital. Or the IDP camp near The City." His shoulders sagged a bit. He was so old, it was hard to believe he had survived all of it. Then again Therese was so young, she could not believe she had survived it either. The sun sank low. They were out of time.

They gave Mr. Muhangi a ride in the big truck back to his schoolhouse inside the church on the Long Road. It was too dangerous for him to be on the lake that close to sunset. They arranged to meet him the next day at the church to interview him again. Therese gave him a big hug and told him she would see him then. As they drove down the highway, Amy unfolded the page of Therese's book from her pocket and handed it to her. She smiled sadly and patted Therese's shoulder.

"You did a great job today," she said. When Therese climbed from the truck to help Olivia with the evening meal, she was more than tired.

CHAPTER NINE

~~~~~~~~~~~~~~

I n the early morning, Therese woke up before Olivia. She lay on her mattress, and her brain went around and around, thinking about all of the people she thought were dead, but who might be alive after all. Because she did not have a telephone or a computer, she could not contact anybody she knew. Even if she did have a computer, how would she find them? Her mind wandered to Mr. Muhangi, to the friends from her village, to Mama, and to Felix. She looked over at the small pile of things she owned: Virgil's bracelet, her journal, the page of her favorite book, and the notes from her brother all sat on the floor next to her mattress. *I am here. Felix.* If only he could write "in the mine" or "with the soldiers," she might have known where to find him. Even two days there made her want to leave. She wanted her family. She needed them. She thought about living her life on the Long Road with Mr. Muhangi. Maybe it would be safe. Maybe Mama and Felix would come back and find them.

A rooster crowed. When Olivia woke up, Therese was already dressed and ready to go. Olivia seemed cross with her. She frowned and told Therese to go help the others with breakfast. She walked to the outhouse and opened the door to find Mwamini holding Giselle over the hole. Her bare bottom was suspended over the pit, and while her mama wiped her, Giselle giggled at Therese.

"Her formula was bad," Mwamini said. A sweet, sour stink reached Therese's nose. Giselle laughed again. It was hot during the day at Brianna's Village. At the hospital there was a cool place to store things like meat and formula, but not there.

"Too bad Olivia doesn't have a refrigerator," Therese said.

Mwamini scowled at her. "Maybe when you're famous, you can buy us one," she said.

"You can't blame me for wanting a better life!" Therese cried.

Mwamini frowned, "There is nothing more. You have these crazy dreams about education and family. There is only this. The cassava field, having babies, and working until we die."

Therese left Mwamini and Giselle in the outhouse to use the bushes behind Olivia's room. As she walked around the sunny side of the cabin, Therese saw why Mwamini was irritated. The Free Child Slaves crew was back. She peered around the corner and saw the FCS truck parked in the shade. Jeff tested a microphone. Thomas talked on his phone in the shadow that his truck cast over him. They looked comfortable, compared to all the girls who hauled cassava and water across the highway. Therese felt guilty that while the other girls had been straining their backs in the hot sun to stay there, she had been driving around in an air-conditioned car with a private driver.

They met Mr. Muhangi at the church on the Long Road. He had kept the place tidy. Jesus still hung on his cross, and the wooden pews shone in neat rows. The windows were dusty, but it was probably because Mr. Muhangi was too short to reach them. Virgil's papa would be so proud to have his church in such good condition. Mr. Muhangi gave Therese hugs and kisses, and she was surprised to see him giving kisses to the film crew too.

"Thank you for telling my story," he said to Amy. Thomas and Therese both translated, but Thomas's translation came out, "Thank you for paying me for telling my story," and Therese looked at him, confused.

"Do you want to show us around?" Amy asked the old man. Jeff handed Therese the camera. They followed Mr. Muhangi to the schoolhouse in the back. It was exactly the same as Papa left it, except Therese's friend had made a small nest for himself in one corner. A few blankets were arranged in a little pile behind the teacher's desk. A slice of sunlight poured in from the window. Therese looked out the glass and saw that his clothes were hung on a line he'd made outside. All the desks that *mzungu* donations bought were lined up in rows. The blackboard was clean.

"I'm proud of this building, and as long as I live, I will keep it clean and ready for students," Mr. Muhangi said. "If there's a church and a school, all of the people from the village will come back someday."

"Are you sure the displaced people from the village and in the hospitals will make their way back?" Amy asked him. Therese could not help but interrupt. She told her, "If they are alive and not stuck in a mine or in a militia, they will come back."

"That's my girl!" said Mr. Muhangi. He was in a much better mood. Therese wondered how much they paid him to be so happy.

"Therese, do you want to return here to live?" asked Amy. Therese was busy shooting Mr. Muhangi's wrinkles in close-up. She was really not sure, and she told her she would come back if she found Mama and Felix. It was nice to be with her friend again. She wanted Virgil to come back too. But a village of five was not enough, and it was unsafe. The bad men would be back to take what they had not yet stolen from them. They would have to build their own little village, away from there, if they wanted to survive.

It was so good to see Mr. Muhangi and to see their lake and village, but she knew she could not live there anymore. As hopeful as she was about seeing her family again, Therese began to doubt their future. She was nervous about where she would go. Before they left, they drove Mr. Muhangi to the other side of the lake to be reunited with the boat he left there the previous night. They said goodbye and promised they would come back for a visit soon. Mr. Muhangi promised Therese again that he would keep the church and the school on the Long Road clean. Therese was glad that someone she loved would always be there to help her find her way back. She worried about him, but she did not think that someone like Mr. Muhangi would ever give up his home. They exchanged kisses, and Therese climbed with the crew back into the truck.

—⟁—

Later in the day, Jeff told Therese that they would not go to the market. The Blue Head men were camped out there, and they'd spotted militia groups nearby. It was too unsafe for them, so they drove instead to the Free Child Slaves office in The City to do some recording of what they called "additional dialogue," which was her voice without pictures. Amy said it would be easier to talk about the market in the office than at the location. Therese did not argue. She did not want to see any bad men. They enjoyed a smooth piece of highway on the way to The City, and Therese asked why the road was so nice.

"The Chinese have a coltan mine up there, and they've paved the road," Jeff said. Therese looked where his finger pointed up the hill on the other side of the highway. The black, smooth pavement snaked up and around and seemed to go on forever. She wondered if a road like that led to Mama and Felix. Amy told her, "Our staff has interviewed many child survivors from the nearby quarries. We have an interview scheduled next week with one of the owners of the mines."

Therese's heart leaped in her chest. "The same mine Robert's brother came from?"

"It is," Amy said. "But it hasn't been an easy interview to get. This man works closely with militia groups. He doesn't like to give interviews, especially to people who may paint him in an unfavor-able light. We had to pay a hefty bribe." They pulled up to a small, white building near The City. Thomas parked the truck. They all climbed out, and Therese followed Jeff up the concrete stairs. There was an armed guard standing there. Amy, Jeff, and Thomas greeted him, "Hello, Mathieu," and he smiled back at them. He was the friendliest-looking man with a gun that Therese had ever seen. She followed them into a long hallway. When Jeff pushed the office door open, posters with children holding pickaxes in front of caves, and children in military uniforms, were all over the walls. A friendly face grinned at her from behind a desk. It was Robert. Her heart fluttered.

"You know Therese, don't you, Robert?" asked Amy. Therese nodded, but what she really wanted to do was hug him. Jeff explained that Robert was doing additional dialogue too. Robert stared at her and smiled again. Amy gave him a playful shove to get his attention.

"All done already?" she asked in French.

Robert nodded and said, "We got everything in one or two takes."

Therese was not following the conversation well. She thought they were talking about using a microphone but was not sure what a "take" was. A young white man with brown hair and bright green eyes came from down the hall wearing headphones that were not plugged into anything.

"I'm Andrew!" he shouted at Therese. He took off his head-phones, rested them on his neck, and offered his hand to her. She'd never before shaken a white man's hand. It felt strange and grown-up, as if she knew something new about the world outside of Congo. Andrew told her that her footage was good. He seemed excited every time he spoke. He was panting a little.

"Andrew's a student from the United States and he's here doing an internship with us," Amy said. Therese nodded as though she knew what that meant. She felt shy in the white person's office, but having Robert there made her feel better. It was the first time since the day her village was burned that she did not want to escape from somewhere. Jeff wrapped up his gum in a tissue, threw it into the trash, and popped another piece into his mouth. It smelled wonderful, like bananas. Therese swallowed hard as he gave Robert a piece. It never occurred to her to ask Jeff for anything.

"No gum when you're doing ADR. You get yours when you finish for the day," Robert told her, winking. Even with a wad of gum in his mouth, he was the handsomest boy she had ever seen.

—‍⁓‍—

Later, in the studio, Robert showed her how to put on the headphones. That was so Andrew and Jeff and Amy could talk to her from the sound room. She sat on a stool in front of a microphone on a stand. Robert sat next to her and watched the footage she shot from Mr. Muhangi's boat play on a screen in front of them. The camera bounced up and down with the current. Therese could see the remains of her village in the distance.

"Therese, just tell us what you see," said Amy.

"Rolling!" said Andrew excitedly.

"This is the view from Mr. Muhangi's boat," she began. "It is very windy, so it is hard to keep the boat straight. We find a bone in the water. I think it is a wild pig's leg, but it is not. It is a person's arm. Mr. Muhangi is angry. I am angry too. This belonged to someone the bad men killed. I think about my Papa and how the bad men cut him up." The narration went on for a bit, with Therese saying what she saw on the screen. More than once she struggled with her tears. Robert took her hand. She was glad to have him there. When they saw where her house used to be, it was hard for Therese to talk. When they saw the cassava field where the bad things happened, Therese could not say anything more.

"Need a break?" asked Amy. Therese looked through the small window into the control room. She had forgotten Amy was there, watching her. Therese could see her backlit hair shining like a fire all around her. She nodded, and the door opened, and fresh air rushed into the studio. Robert climbed down from his stool. He smiled at Therese and whispered, "I understand how hard it is to relive bad memories."

They all went into a large meeting room for their lunch. There were maps on every wall with colored thumbtacks stuck into them.

On one map, Therese saw a large circle that looked like their volcano. She also saw a large lake, and she knew by its shape that her home was near it. On what looked like a snaking highway, many red and yellow thumbtacks stuck out about a finger's length away from her village. She turned to Robert, who nodded at her.

"That's where your brother is," he said. Therese sucked in her breath. The adults were busy setting out lunch. Amy opened a box full of fried fish and set it on the table, and Thomas brought bottles of water. Jeff spoke with Andrew about how good the footage was.

"Are they paying you yet?" asked Robert. She shook her head, and he said, "Don't give them anything else until they give you something back."

She told him that they were already paying Olivia to have Therese stay with her.

"But when they finish their film, what then?" he asked. "What happens to you when they're done?" Therese didn't know.

"They'll find my family for me. That's enough. Isn't it?"

"No, it's not. You need money. You need an education. You need a home!" he hissed. He seemed angry with her. She did not know what to say. She thought Olivia was giving her everything she needed.

"What if I they don't give me any money?" Therese asked him.

Robert said, "There's a big donor due to visit in a few days. I'll see what I can do." He could tell she was nervous. Robert punched her lightly in the arm and said, "Don't worry, you're their star. There's no movie without you."

"Lunch is ready!" called Andrew. He seemed very young. Maybe he was just a few years older than Robert. How did someone so young move around the world if they had not had a chance to earn much money? Surely he had wealthy parents or a great education. She followed Andrew and Robert to the table. She had never seen so much food. The Americans ate their fish with forks and knives. They were delicate about putting the metal in their mouths. Amy, however, picked hers up with her hands and ate it like an African. She sucked the bones clean, the way Thomas, Robert, and Therese did.

—ɷ—

After several rounds of narrating in English, her brain needed a break. Robert had gone to be with his aunt and uncle for the evening. Therese felt sad when he left. The fluttery feeling she had in her heart when he was around disappeared when he went away. Therese did not want to go back to Brianna's Village again. She wanted to stay in The City, near Virgil and Robert. But she had to go back and work, or Olivia would not let her stay.

On the drive back down the highway, Therese sat in the back seat and chewed the delicious gum that Robert asked Jeff to give to her. It tasted as good as it smelled. She looked at The Volcano out the window and thought about Mama. She missed the colors of her *kanga*, and the scent of mango lotion she breathed in when she hugged her. She missed the way she rubbed Therese's back to help her fall asleep when her mind was busy thinking. She missed the veins on her hand and the soft brown skin that covered them. Talking to Robert taught her to not be okay with things that were not right. She missed her family, and that was not right.

CHAPTER TEN

T he next day was special because Brianna, the woman who started the village for Olivia, would be visiting. The girls were busy cleaning up and tidying their rooms because she would bring gifts to them. Olivia's deep dimples were showing.

Brianna arrived in a truck that had a picture on the door of a gun with a slash across it. She was surprised that Brianna arrived alone. Most white people had a local driver to help them around, but this *mzungu* was brave. Brianna stepped from the driver's seat. She was a tiny, skinny, brown-haired woman, and when she exited the car, Olivia embraced her like family. Both women immediately started to cry while they hugged. Brianna sneezed and apologized that her nose was not used to so much dust. All the children gathered around her truck. Olivia pulled the kids away, but that only caused them to swarm around their visitor. Brianna put her arms around them. Therese stood a little distance away, unsure of what to do, until Olivia called her over. She introduced them, and when Therese extended her hand, Brianna took it in both of hers. Therese felt special already.

Olivia asked her to translate.

"*Jambo!*" Brianna said to the group.

"*Jambo sana!*" the whole group said back.

"A very big welcome to you, Brianna!" Therese said.

"I've brought you some gifts this time, but I'd like to hear your news first," Brianna said. "May we speak inside?"

Therese hoped her translation was good. This was an important person, and Therese needed her to think she was an important girl. The entire group moved in the direction of the lean-to. Brianna turned to her.

"Your English is beautiful. Where did you learn it?"

She told Brianna that Mama had been teaching her English her entire life. Brianna shook her head as if she could not believe her.

"What a gift she gave you," she said. Therese watched the children follow her, almost tripping on her heels. She wore flip-flops, which was different than all the other *mzungu* Therese had seen wearing sneakers and other closed-toed shoes. She told Brianna that she liked her flip-flops. She wondered if Brianna wore closed shoes in America.

"The first time I came here, I was in sneakers," Brianna said. "One of the girls asked me why I got to wear closed shoes when she was in bare feet."

"I think you should wear what you want," Therese offered.

"You remind me of my kids when I try to tell them what to wear," she said, laughing. Brianna put her hand into her purse and pulled out her wallet. Brianna took out two pictures, one of a boy with blond hair who was about five, and a little guy who looked to be three. The baby looked just like Brianna. Therese wanted to ask her why she left her boys to come there and speak with them, but instead, she said, "Maybe someday I can meet them."

"I think that's a great idea," Brianna said. She put her arm around Therese, as if it were the easiest thing to hug a stranger. Therese felt like she was walking with Mama. She was curious about this *mzungu*. She wanted to know more about her.

They went into the lean-to. Immediately Giselle plopped down at Brianna's feet. She examined the toes of the donor. Her nails were painted red, the color of blood; the toddler touched them and looked to Brianna's face. Brianna smiled at Giselle, but the baby looked concerned. Mwamini seated herself next to the donor and said, "She thinks you have hurt yourself," pointing to her blood-colored toes. Therese translated, and Brianna laughed.

"Will you tell her it's only paint?" she asked Therese. She told Giselle, who then giggled and petted Brianna's toes. Mwamini frowned at Therese.

"It's only paint," Therese repeated for Mwamini. Her frown got deeper as Therese held the lean-to open for Hiroute. Her black eyes had faded to a normal color, and her gaze was pointed at the gravelly ground. She covered her toothless smile with her hand. Without those missing teeth, she would be very pretty. Olivia sat on the other side of the donor and introduced Hiroute.

Brianna looked at Hiroute's broken smile, and her eyes began to fill. And that was how the meeting started, with the new girls telling their stories. Therese translated for everybody. She explained that Hiroute's husband almost killed her after she had been raped. About how Mwamini and Giselle were thrown out of their village after they were attacked. And about herself. Hiroute and Therese had something in common. Neither girl had to carry a baby around with them. But as she looked at her, Therese realized that she had open sores on her face. She was sick to a point that she could not be helped in a hospital anymore. Was this going to be the final stop for her? No more treatment? Just AIDS? Then there was Mwamini, who was young and strong, but had to carry Giselle with her wherever she went. Therese wondered which was worse, not knowing if your family was alive, or knowing your family would never take you back. Would Mama still love Therese even though she was raped? And what if she was still taking medicine from what the bad man did? Would Mama still take her back? Her head started to spin. She felt the walls of the lean-to start to suck in and out with her breath, and Therese excused herself to go outside.

Before she knew what was happening, Therese was standing beside the outhouse, crying. She felt panic rising in her, and the fear that she would be left there at Olivia's compound, without Mama, without Felix or Mr. Muhangi or Robert, without Amy or Brianna, away from people who could help her.

Brianna ran out of the lean-to after her. When she saw her tears, she put her arms around her and pulled her close. Therese could smell the sweat of the inside of the hot lean-to on her. She felt terrible for ruining her donor visit like that but couldn't seem to stop sobbing.

"Therese, don't cry," Brianna soothed her. She hummed a sweet-sounding song and rocked her back and forth.

"I want my mama. I want my family. I want it to go back to normal like before the bad men came." Therese sobbed.

"I know, Therese. I'm so sorry." Tears spilled from her eyes too.

Suddenly Therese was angry. "You will cry your white person's tears now and then go back home and forget about me!" she said, wailing. She could feel Brianna flinch at her words.

"I could never forget you," Brianna said. She lifted her chin with one finger and stared into her eyes. "Do you hear me, Therese?" She nodded miserably.

They heard everyone leaving the lean-to. They all glared at Therese as they headed toward Brianna's truck. Olivia approached them and put her hand on Therese's shoulder. Therese continued to gaze into Brianna's eyes, wondering how much she could trust her. Brianna nodded toward the truck, took her hand, and said, "Let's go help them."

Brianna, Olivia, and Therese walked to the truck. Brianna hauled out two enormous duffel bags. She handed out pencils and clothing to everyone. Giselle jumped up and grabbed a stuffed animal out of her hand. "It's going to be okay," said Olivia, patting Therese's back.

After Brianna left, Therese was exhausted from her outburst. She did not think she was still able to cry about everything that had happened. It had been so long. Why did she feel so weepy? In her room, she spread the new pencils and clothes she received from Brianna on the bed. She decided to try on a dress. It had a black background with little pink flowers on it. They were the first new clothes she had gotten in a long time. The dress had a long waist that rested on her hips. She touched the cotton under her hands, the soft, clean fabric on her chest. Something was different. She felt two small bumps under her hands. Mama would probably cry because she was growing up so fast. Even though Therese saw things happening all around her, she never thought of the changes in her own body. She looked at the pile of new clothes, and instead of trying on the rest, she grabbed a pencil. Therese sat on her mattress and dug out her journal. Her words flowed easily, but she did not have much time. Olivia came in, looking nervous.

"You need to come outside for good reception!" she said. Therese followed her, not knowing what that meant. They walked past all the girls in their new dresses. Olivia handed her phone to her. She helped Therese put it to her ear. She'd never used a cell phone before. Olivia put her hands on her round hips and smiled at her.

"Hello, Therese?" said Amy.

"Yes! I am Therese!" she yelled into the phone.

"We have something for you," she said. Therese heard a smile in Amy's voice. She waited, not knowing if it might be money or maybe a promise of an education. She sweated in her new dress.

"We found Felix, and he's alive," Amy started to say, but Therese did not let her finish. She sank to her knees, clapped her hands loudly, and held them up to Heaven. The phone was away from her ear now, but she could hear Amy say something about "negotiating his release" and a hospital stay. God was good, just like Mr. Muhangi said. God was so good! She had a family again! She was not alone in the world. Therese put the phone back to her ear.

"Is he okay?" Therese asked. She could picture Amy holding a telephone, smiling with her twinkly blue eyes. She said if Felix had been injured, he would need medical care.

"When can I see him?" Therese asked her. She waited a bit before answering. Amy explained, "They still need to transport him from the mine in an ambulance," which worried Therese. Amy said, "You're not allowed to see him until we know how bad his injuries are. As long as we're just waiting, would you come into the office?"

"I don't want to go until I see Felix," Therese said simply. They probably wanted her back in the studio because of the new changes. Now it was her turn to wait before answering. She thought about the bumps under her dress and about how soon it would be that she would be in danger of having a baby. Therese did not want to be raped again and get stuck at Brianna's Village forever. She felt uncomfortable in her skin, like it was a curse to have been born a girl. She slouched in her dress, thinking everyone could see her new body. Without Mama there, Therese did not know what to do. Felix was going to be free soon, and he would need someone to take care of him.

"I need you to pay me, so I can support Felix," she said, like a mama.

"Okay," Amy said. Therese could not believe it. Felix and payment all in one day! She handed the phone to Olivia, who would not let her listen to the rest of her conversation. She smiled at Therese and pointed to the rest of the group. It was almost mealtime, and the others had put pots of water over cook fires to boil. Therese stood up straighter. She could not hide her joy, striding in her new dress, knowing Felix was alive, and she would have money of her own. All the other girls looked so pretty. They were smiling also. She would not tell them about the money or about Felix. Therese had learned to keep her mouth shut.

It was April, and almost Therese's twelfth birthday. Many rainy days had gone by, and she still had not seen Felix. The FCS crew was interviewing a man named The Mole, the brother of The General, whose men took Mama and Felix and so many others from her village. The Congolese Army had arrested The Mole for crimes against humanity. The Mole owned the mine where Felix was taken. He told Amy that because Felix was so small, he could not properly hold a gun, so when The Mole learned he could speak English and French, he made him his official translator. It seemed that Mama's gifts had kept Felix alive too.

Amy said it would take time for Felix to be well enough for a visit, but Therese never knew it would take so long. She was also sad to hear that Olivia would be the one holding onto Therese's payments from FCS. Olivia said that Therese was too young to be trusted with her own money. The dry ground at Olivia's house had given way to mud. The girls and Therese slipped around in their flip-flops. With every drop of rain that fell, Therese got more and more nervous, and it was raining a lot.

Brianna had given a big donation of money to Olivia. Now Olivia had the girls planting some new crops of corn. Her cassava was no longer enough for the girls there. Her plan was to build a bigger place for her chickens too. Therese was glad that Olivia was doing well, but she did not want to be there anymore. Therese wanted to take Felix, find Mama, and go far, far away. As she bent over the little trench in the soil and dropped a corn seed into the ground, Therese studied the wet soil. It was a dark red. The corn would sprout underground and grow roots. It would grow there, tall and green, like a big grass. When it was time to be picked, someone would put it into a basket and cart it off. Therese had been growing too. Her feet sank in the mud. Under her second-hand jacket, she felt herself getting tall and changing. If she could only be picked up and carted off too.

Finally, one day, the FCS truck pulled up in the mud in front of Olivia's house. Therese looked up from her planting and wiped the mud out of her eyes. There was a storm cloud overhead, but the rain had stopped for the moment. She dropped her sack of seeds and stepped over Couchou the cat, who jumped onto the sack and sharpened her claws on it. Olivia met Amy at the truck with a large umbrella. As Therese went closer, she saw that there was someone other than the normal crew inside. Robert rolled his window down and waved. Therese had not seen him for so long that she smiled a big smile.

"It's a good day, Therese," said Amy. Her hair hung down like a wet, red mop. She handed Olivia a large envelope. Olivia squeezed Therese's shoulder. Amy told Therese that Felix was awake and ready for visitors. Her blue eyes swam in tears behind her glasses. Therese could not control herself and threw her arms around Amy. She knew Jeff was rolling from inside the truck. She did not care that she was covered in mud up to her knees. The camera could have it.

Therese could not believe they could all fit in the truck. Thomas and Amy were in the front. Jeff sat in the back. Nobody could sit next to him without one of his knees stabbing them in the thigh. The side-facing seats in the far back were reserved for Robert and Therese. It was hard for Robert to balance in the seat because he had only the one leg. He braced his cane on the floor when they went around turns. It was a dangerous drive. It was rainy, muddy, and getting toward dusk. That was when the militia groups came out. Any car on the road could be taken over at a roadblock. Therese watched Robert as he looked out the window. She noticed again what a beautiful face he had. His cheekbones were high and his nose had a bit of a bump in it, like a hawk. Therese felt strange about Robert. He was growing and changing too. He seemed like a man to her. She caught him staring at her. Suddenly he jumped up and pointed out the window behind Therese.

"Look at that village!" he shouted. They all looked. In the distance, one of the small towns near The City had fallen into a lake. The first line of buildings had slid on the mud into the water. There were mothers screaming for their children. A large fire was burning in the second line of buildings, and a house exploded as they drove by.

"Stop the car! We have to help!" Therese yelled. As the words came out of her mouth, a green jeep with machine guns mounted on it sped by them toward the village. Instead of slowing down, Thomas sped up toward The City.

"It's not safe, Therese," Jeff said. Thomas was already on his telephone, giving directions to someone. Therese did not understand. How could it be unsafe to help others? Jeff leaned over to the window to shoot the scene. Then Therese saw it: In front of them, a roadblock had been set up. Men in mismatched uniforms stood in front of it, pointing their machine guns as they approached. Amy dug around in her bag and pulled out her passport. Therese heard Thomas say something into his phone about another camera. She sweated in the air conditioning. Something about this felt wrong. Usually, when there was a roadblock, it was the Blue Head men trying to keep people from driving too fast on a washed-out road. Thomas hid his phone and put his hand out to Jeff and Amy, who handed him their passports. Jeff hid the camera on the floor.

Therese shook because she thought she recognized one of the men. She could not be sure, but she thought he was about the same age as the bad man from the cassava field, the one who attacked her. The spit in her mouth dried up fast. He smiled at her through the window. Robert grabbed her hand and they stared into each other's eyes. Thomas rolled down his window. A man with a necklace of human teeth grabbed the passports out of his hands and looked at all of them. The bad man from the cassava field said, "Give me that camera, and then you can go."

"We'll pay you later," said Amy, in French. Therese could not believe she was talking like that to a man with a gun. She was either very brave or very stupid. Thomas translated, and the bad man said, "Shut up, fat boy!"

The other bad man said, "You pay us now, or we take those kids with us," and Jeff handed him the camera with a sigh. The man with the necklace of human teeth threw the passports back in Thomas's face. Thomas drove through the roadblock toward The City. His meaty hands shook as they gripped the steering wheel.

Robert still clutched Therese's hand. His arm was so rigid, she was afraid he might crush her fingers. If those were The General's men, they would view Robert as a deserter. He was probably as nervous as she was. Therese struggled to read his eyes. Instead of fear, she saw fury. He looked so strong, and his eyes gave her strength.

"It's okay, Therese," Amy told them.

"I lose more cameras that way!" said Jeff jokingly. He passed everyone a piece of watermelon gum. Therese could not open it because her hands were shaking so hard. Thomas gave Amy and Jeff their passports. As relieved as she was about getting through the roadblock, Therese had a feeling she would not be returning to Olivia's that night. They slipped their way through The City. Many trucks were sliding in the red mud. A large van was stuck in the middle of the street. The weight of all the passengers inside made it sink deeper into the mud. There were hundreds of locals out on the street. It was strange to see so many people on the side of the road after being out in farmland so long. Several people carried umbrellas or had hoods on their jackets. The ones who did not have jackets ducked under the awnings of stores to stay out of the rain. They pulled up to the large volcanic-rock wall of the hospital and honked. A Blue Head guard opened the heavy, metal door. As they pulled in, Therese felt the hospital's strong wall around her, and with Robert's hand on hers, she felt safe again.

There was another FCS truck in the driveway. The armed guard from the FCS office smiled at them through the truck's window and held out another camera to Amy and Jeff. Robert and Therese peered through the rain to the hospital. Therese half expected to see Odette and Esther, but she remembered that since she was last there, they had probably moved on, Esther to New Beginnings and Odette to a high school in France. Therese did not have time to miss them. She was going to see Felix. In the front archway, Valentin greeted them. He held two umbrellas in the rainy darkness of the night. Therese gave him a big hug, and she followed him into the large lobby.

CHAPTER ELEVEN

"Look how tall you are, Therese!" said Dr. Bingi when he saw her. She crossed her arms over her breasts to hide them. She was embarrassed but could not help grinning because she knew Felix was nearby. Dr. Bingi's strong arms held her and kept her warm for a minute.

"Therese!" sang Desanges. She was more beautiful and browner than Therese remembered. Desanges took her wet fleece and hung it on a hook behind her desk in the lobby. Therese turned to Amy and asked, "Does Jeff need to film this?" She told Therese, "Why don't you go ahead? We'll catch up with you soon."

Therese looked at Robert and he nodded. Somehow they all knew that it was private between Felix and Therese. She followed Valentin's broad back and again noticed the militia tattoo on his arm. Therese wondered if Felix would have one and she felt concerned that getting a tattoo might have hurt him. Dr. Bingi took her hand and escorted Therese down the hall and into the courtyard. Because of the rain, the playground was empty; everyone was eating inside the cafeteria. Therese was hungry, but she could not even think of food. She asked how Felix was.

"He was weak and hungry when he arrived. He slept a lot. His stomach is swollen from poor food, so he has an IV drip. And he had lice, so we shaved his head. Felix has two broken fingers, but other than that, his body is okay. You should know, Therese, that the night you were attacked, he was also attacked. He is lucky to be alive, but his heart is very troubled. Felix is going to need to spend some extra time here. Do you understand?"

She nodded but did not understand. She thought about the white and red that had come from between her own legs. Could this happen to a boy? Doctor Bingi interrupted her thoughts before they went too far.

"He's not carrying any other illness, thank God. He'll be happy to see you, but please go slow with him, Therese," he said. Valentin opened a door to a recovery room and gently said, "Felix, you have a visitor."

Therese could not believe what she saw. There, tiny, pregnant looking, was Felix. He stared at her with eyes too enormous for his face. His smile was gone, but she could tell he recognized her. He had a tube in one arm, and the other arm was propped up on a pillow. Two fingers were taped to a metal and foam splint. His elbows were giant compared to his skinny arms, but it was Felix. She could not move. There was her family. The only one besides Therese. Valentin took her hand and walked her over to Felix. Dr. Bingi gave her a little push from behind.

Therese sat on his bedside and kissed his bony cheeks. She bent over his small form and pressed her chest to his. He did not hug back, but she could not seem to pull herself from him. She wrapped her arms around his skinny body and inhaled. Even though he smelled of hospital soap, she recognized him. She started to babble a stream of I-love-you-my-brother-my-brother. Therese felt his heart thump against hers. She breathed him in through her nose and out her mouth. She felt him shift beneath her weight, like she was hurting him, and she lifted up a bit. His ribs poked into hers, and his tummy felt as if he had a soccer ball inside of it. Doctor Bingi said, "Stay as long as you want."

Valentin pulled a chair over to the side of the bed for her to sit on. Therese heard approaching sirens outside. They were probably injured people arriving from the burning village. Valentin and Dr. Bingi quickly slipped out the door. She looked closely at Felix. His hair was gone. There was a rash on his head from where he had scratched the lice. Scabs stuck up from his scalp like tiny islands. The whites of his eyes had rivers of red passing through them, as if he had not slept for a long, long time. He sighed and his eyes got heavy. Therese watched the pulse bump up and down in his neck. She put her hand on the soft, clean gown on his chest. Her baby brother was alive. She had a family again. Therese ran her hand down and placed it on his belly. He used to let her tickle him there, but now, he stopped her hand with his own. The cold splint on his broken fingers shocked her a little. He was so changed since he'd been gone. *Maybe he does not trust me,* she worried. She stood up from the bed, afraid to touch him then, and moved to the chair, but he patted the bed next to him, so she sat back down on his mattress. His eyes got heavy again and he started to fall asleep. She watched him like that for a while. Therese felt comfortable just hearing his breath. She realized how tired she was. She slipped off her flip-flops, moved the pillow under his hand, and climbed under his thin blankets. For the first time in weeks, she curled herself around him. He woke up for a minute and whispered, "I am here."

CHAPTER TWELVE

Everything changed when Felix came back. Instead of working half the day for Olivia at Brianna's Village and going into The City for additional dialogue recording, Therese had a new job as caretaker for Felix. She woke early, helped with Olivia's morning meal, and immediately went in the FCS truck to visit her brother. He was doing much better; he could eat solid foods and get out of his bed. He was still a bit wobbly on his legs, so he used a wheelchair. Virgil visited him every day too. The fracture in Virgil's leg was on the growth plate, so he would need an additional surgery to repair it. He would get to stay at the hospital with Felix even longer. Virgil was a source of great friendship for Felix. Valentin let them visit way past hours, but Virgil often got in trouble for bringing a soccer ball to Felix's bed.

Therese borrowed a wheelchair and rolled Felix out to the courtyard to watch Virgil play soccer. Virgil's armpits had developed callouses from all his soccer playing on crutches, but still, he was at a disadvantage against the other kids. Felix looked on quietly from his wheelchair, and when Virgil asked him to play, he did not want to. Her brother seemed very sad to her. Mama and Papa named him Felix because he was such a happy baby. But he thought serious things all the time. Therese helped him walk around his room, but he was very weak. In group meeting, when Dr. Bingi asked him to speak about what happened in the mine, all he would do was pull his short tufts of regrown hair. Thank goodness it was so short that he could not pull it all the way out. The doctor told Therese that was Felix's way of organizing his feelings. To be able to control his own hair was a way of controlling his life. That did not make any sense to her, someone pulling at his own hair, eyebrows, and eyelashes to put his life in order.

When they met with Dr. Bingi for group therapy, Amy sometimes stopped in. She and Jeff asked Felix questions about Mama. They thought that Mama was still with The General. But every time they asked Felix about her, he pulled at his eyebrows. Sometimes Therese wanted to shake him. Terrible things happened to them, but they all survived. If she could make a film and talk about it, he could surely answer a few questions to help find Mama. But then Therese remembered that he was so little, and she felt bad.

When he was strong enough, Felix would share a room with Virgil. That made Therese very happy. It was like a promise that Felix would be out of the hospital soon. But then where would he go? Brianna's Village? Olivia could not afford to take care of anybody else. And even though most boys in Congo went to school, for those with little money, school was too expensive.

Robert came to see Therese at the hospital almost every day. He'd been busy trying to get someone to sponsor him to go to high school. Therese thought that since he had family close by, there would be money to send him to school, but since the bad men came and took everything, nobody had any money. Robert seemed as though he could do anything. Therese could not imagine he would not find a sponsor. Almost every day, she walked out the front door with him. They sat in the parking lot, and Therese kept him company while he smoked a cigarette. It was a habit he picked up while working for the militia. Robert looked a little strange with a cigarette sticking out of his mouth. He was too young to smoke, Therese thought.

"You aren't with the bad men anymore. Why do you still do it?" she asked.

"I don't know, but I'll quit soon," he told her. Therese looked at where his pant leg was cut off just under the knee.

"Maybe you'll quit when your leg grows back," she told him, and he laughed. Therese thought about Felix pulling out his hair and not knowing why he did it. A habit was a habit, no matter how it got there.

—✺—

Brianna arrived one day, and in the sharing center she announced, "I have a plan to sponsor three special girls to go to the school at New Beginnings for a six-month training session."

Therese had a fluttery feeling in her belly. If she was selected, she would learn so much there. She could learn computers, self-defense, and maybe even find a way into high school.

"New Beginnings is all the way on the other end of The City's Lake, which is as big as an ocean. It's a big commitment, and a big opportunity," said Brianna. It would be so far from The City, which sat on the northern edge of the lake, near the border with Rwanda. New Beginnings would be like a new life for Therese. But then, she thought about Felix and Virgil. If she left them, what would they do? And what about Robert? Her stomach gave a little jump when she thought about him. She loved the hook in his nose, the flatness of his cheeks, and his straight, white teeth when he smiled. She imagined the cigarette in his mouth and thought about his lips on hers.

When she went to the river to wash, Therese noticed a strange, musky smell coming from her underarms. It was a warm, ripe smell. She looked at her own body. There was a bit of fuzz between her legs and under her arms. Was this what it meant to be a woman? What would she do when her periods started? If Mama were there, she would help Therese with that. Suddenly she realized that it was almost May. She had a birthday in early April, and nobody knew. Mama and Papa never let a birthday go by without a celebration and a new book for Therese. She dried off with a long, colored rectangle of cloth and then wrapped it around her waist.

She pulled on a tank top and tucked it in tight. Without Mama, Therese did not know if she was ready to be a woman.

Her spoken English was getting stronger by the day. Because she wrote her journal in English, she felt connected to other people who spoke the language. Every time Brianna came by for a visit, she spoke with her. Brianna showed her recent pictures of her boys. Therese had noticed some of the babies there wearing the clothes that used to belong to Brianna's family. Therese was wearing donated clothes too. It was so strange, speaking English, wearing American clothes. It seemed as if she were reaching out from Africa, all the way to another continent. She remembered also feeling that way back with her family, when they read old, donated books in English or French.

Therese greeted Brianna in English, and always with a smile. She had the idea that if she went to New Beginnings, maybe Brianna and Olivia would let Felix and Virgil stay at the village. Olivia often asked how Felix was doing. Therese told her that he was much better, how special he was, and how Virgil and he were such close friends. Therese needed for Olivia to let them come there. She didn't want either of them to end up in an Internally Displaced People's camp. Therese wanted them to go to school and have a safe place to stay.

One day Therese went to visit the hospital with the FCS crew and discovered that it was moving day for Felix. He was going to share a room with Virgil. While Jeff shot her walking across the courtyard to meet him, Therese narrated.

"He will be much happier with our unbrother. It is not so much fun having Valentin and Desanges checking on you all the time . . ." she said. Jeff and Amy seemed distracted. Therese wondered if they had lost interest in her story, now that Felix and she were safe. Amy's cell phone rang, and she walked off with it tucked under her giant red hair, with the boom microphone in the other hand. Therese still had Jeff's attention, at least, as they walked toward the medical building. Desanges stood up behind her desk and went with them to see Felix.

In his room, Felix sat up in bed. He ate what looked like a normal meal: cassava leaves and rice and a little fish. The tube in his arm was gone, and he looked a lot better to Therese. She went in and hugged him, and when she turned around, Jeff was gone. Desanges and Therese let Felix finish lunch before getting him settled into Virgil's room. It looked a lot like Therese's old room that she shared with Odette. Virgil had a small collection of treasures, just as she did. He had a soccer ball near his bed, and several pictures hung on his wall, including a poster of the Ethiopian soccer team. Felix's side of the room was mostly bare. Secondhand clothes were stacked on the dresser, and clean sheets sat in a pile on his bed. Desanges held Felix by the elbow and helped him into a chair.

"Where is Virgil?" he asked. Therese jumped a little at the question. Felix had been so quiet that she'd almost forgotten how his voice sounded.

"He is being examined by Dr. Bingi, so they can figure out when to schedule the surgery for his leg," Desanges told him. There was a knock on the door, and when Therese opened it, Robert was standing there. She smiled at him, but he looked so serious, she did not say anything.

"Hi, little man," he said to Felix, who smiled at him in a shy way. Felix always loved older boys, and he was interested in Robert, who seemed wise and strong. Robert turned to Therese and said, "We need to talk."

Therese left Desanges making Felix's bed and followed Robert outside, into the courtyard. The sky looked darker, and the air smelled of metal and rain. She asked him where FCS went, and he told her that there was a raid by the Congolese Army. Big, fat raindrops began to fall on them. She looked into Robert's eyes and could see that there was more.

"What else?" she asked him. He pressed his lips together and took a big breath.

"The General is on the run. He fled into the bush and looks like he's going to cross the lake. A bunch of NGOs are tracking him, and they found lots of women on the roadside . . ."

"My mama?" Therese blurted out.

Robert readjusted his cane, so he did not sink in the mud. She could feel her flip-flops being sucked down, and she was a little unsteady. It was hot and sticky outside, even though the rain kept falling. She sweated and shivered at the same time.

"I don't know," he said. "I'm going back to the FCS office where I can listen in and I'll tell you anything I hear." He patted her gently on the back. A shock ran through her when he touched her. Therese felt nervous about Mama and excited at being so close to Robert, all at the same time. She watched him leave and was amazed by how he got around with only one leg and a cane, especially in the mud and rain. She stood in the downpour watching him and thinking about the other side of the lake. Aside from New Beginnings, she had not heard of anything on the other side. Why was The General going there? If Therese went across the lake with the FCS crew, would that get her closer to Mama? She looked toward Felix's dorm and thought about staying close to her brother. Then she glanced up at the volcanic rock wall that surrounded the hospital. It was topped all around by razor wire. Felix was safe there, even without her.

"Robert!" Therese yelled. He turned to face her. "Can I come with you?"

—⁓—

It was the first time she had ever been one of the people walking on the road in The City. Until then she had always been in a bus with Papa or in the FCS truck. The ruts in the road slowed traffic to a stop, and everything that stopped in the mud pretty much stayed there or slid off to the side. Therese felt lucky to be on foot, but there were so many people walking that passing each other without being hit by a sliding car was difficult.

They passed the statue of golden *chucadu*. The rickshaw cycle was everywhere in The City. Anybody who did not carry a load on their head transported their load on the wooden cycle. She stepped aside as a small boy slowly scooted his stack of charcoal past them on one. The FCS office was not far from the hospital, but in the rain, it took them nearly an hour to get there. When they finally arrived, they were splattered in mud. Their footprints followed them up the stairs. The armed guard said, "Welcome back," to Therese. They opened the office door and heard Andrew screaming into the phone.

"I understand, Jeff, but if it's not going, I can't get you another ticket. We have to wait until . . ."

He gestured out the window at the lake. Therese never noticed before how close it was. The water churned in the storm and it looked like an ocean from there. She could not see the docks in the foreground, but Therese knew that the boats must be bumping against each other. Andrew hung up the phone. Therese asked him what happened. Before she knew it, she was translating for Robert and Andrew in Swahili and English.

"It's too rough for the express boat to Port Town," Andrew explained. "They can't cross until the storm blows over. Jeff and Amy are at the dock, and Jeff's pissed. They really want to see if The General is still there. They don't even know if he left anyone to rescue. There's nothing I can do."

"Can they take the express boat tomorrow?" asked Robert. Andrew shook his head and said, "It runs every other day. The only one left today is the slow boat, but it's pretty rough, and it'll get them there a full day later."

Therese could barely follow all the discussion about boats, but she knew that if they were crossing the lake, she wanted to go with them. She heard heavy footsteps coming up the stairs. Out in the hall, Thomas and the armed guard smoked cigarettes and joked about the *mzungu* film crew and how impatient they were. Andrew looked to Therese for a translation. She shrugged and told him, "You would not understand. It is an African thing."

It was the first time she lied during a translation. The wind pounded against the glass and pushed cold air under the door. She looked at the map of The City's Lake on the wall. The lake was huge. On the other end of the water was the town called Port Town. There was a green pin stuck into it and a big circle around the town. The distance between The City and Port Town was great and there were several islands in between. Therese wondered about people on the islands. How did they cross the lake in such a big storm? It was too far to swim, and motorboats were expensive. The door downstairs flung open in the wind, and clomping boots raced up the stairs. Jeff and Amy stared at her from the doorway, dripping in their foul weather gear. Covered from head to foot, they looked like yellow trash bags. Therese smiled at them, but they looked angry.

"What are you doing here!" demanded Jeff. He was so mad that she could not answer. Therese had a sudden cramp in her stomach and wondered if she was getting sick.

"You're supposed to be at the hospital with your brother, aren't you?" asked Amy. She started peeling off her wet, yellow layers. Her hair, matted down with rain, stuck to her face. Therese realized that in the short months since her village was attacked, they had become responsible for her, as she had become responsible for Felix. They did not like that she left the safety of the hospital with Robert. Therese felt bad for making them worry.

"If you take me across the lake with you, I will never leave your side, and you can watch me all the time. Even film me . . ." she said.

"We aren't running a taxi service here, Therese. Do you know how hard it is to get across the lake?" Jeff snapped.

"Not to mention the money," Amy added. Outside in the hall, Therese overheard Thomas say, ". . . back and forth to Olivia's . . ."

and she really felt guilty. She started to understand that they were using up their money to get her from Olivia's to the hospital every day.

Robert walked into the hallway where he could talk in his native tongue and stay out of the trouble she was in. Alone in a room full of Americans, Therese tried to think like one. What would an impatient person do in that situation? She thought about the Blue Head men in their fancy vehicles. They seemed to get around pretty well.

"Does the UN have a big boat? Maybe they can get us a ride across?" Therese suggested.

"Great idea, but the UN has already taken their boat across," Amy told her. "It's on the other side of the lake." She tapped her watch at Jeff.

"Why don't you give us a chance to think about this, Therese," he said. "There's nothing for you to do here until the weather clears. We'll be in contact with you once we know something. Thomas will take you back to Olivia's." Jeff turned his back on her, as if the conversation were done.

"But I do not want to go back to Olivia's!" she yelled. Therese did not want to be ignored. "Mama is out there!" she screamed. "She might be with The General! I need to get across that lake!"

Robert stuck his head back through the door and motioned for her to come into the hallway.

"You need to get their attention, but this isn't the way," he counseled her. He squeezed her shoulder. Therese's anger had risen into her cheeks, and her heart raced because he was touching her again. She could not believe he grinned at her at a time like that. It made her warm and angry all over again. Thomas cleared his throat. Therese forgot he was in the hallway with Robert.

"We'd better go, Therese. That storm isn't getting any weaker," Thomas said.

—⁓—

Thomas dropped her off at Olivia's. Therese was outraged to be back. What was she doing there?

"Where have you been? You haven't worked in days!" Olivia thundered. "We need to all contribute, if we're going to survive here!"

"I'm sorry, Olivia. I just want more than that," said Therese. She left Olivia standing in the rain, staring after her. She could get on that boat and find Mama herself. She could take some food, rain gear, a machete, and a flashlight, and walk to Mr. Muhangi's home in the church on the Long Road. Maybe from there, she could take the bus she once took with Papa into The City. Mr. Muhangi was not that far away. If FCS would not take Therese across, couldn't she just go alone? Would he give her some money? Before she realized what she was doing, Therese grabbed the flashlight off Olivia's nightstand. She changed into a new dress with many pockets. She put the flashlight in one of the pockets and slipped on an old donated yellow raincoat. Therese went to the cook stoves and tried to look like she was helping make lunch, but she really spent most of her time filling up her pockets with food. She piled her plate high with beans and meat. She found a spot under an awning and ate as much as she could. To her surprise, Mwamini sat next to her. Giselle toddled over through the rain too.

"What are you doing?" Mwamini asked. Therese told her that she was eating lunch. Mwamini looked at her suspiciously.

"What's in your pocket?" she asked. Therese told her it was a flashlight, so that she could find her way around, in case the power went out in the storm. Mwamini stuck out her hand from under the awning. She said it was a terrible rain and that she would not want to be traveling in it. Therese tried to swallow the food, but she just chewed and chewed. She looked out into the rain, which the wind blew sideways. Giselle nibbled a banana and began to cry when the wind blew the peel into her mouth. While Mwamini was distracted, Therese got up to stoke the cook fire.

She did not return to her. Therese stuffed as much food into her mouth as she could, left her plate, and went around to the back to the tool shed. She took a machete and hid it under her raincoat. She crossed the bridge to the fields, as if going to work, but she just kept going, through the fields, until she reached the highway. She could not see Olivia's house from there. The fields hid her from it, and it from her. In flip-flops, she ran through the terrible storm on the highway. Therese did not know how long it would take to get to Mr. Muhangi's house and didn't care. She was leaving to find Mama and would walk as long as it took. Therese pulled the machete from her coat and slung it over her shoulder. She hoped that the fruit she stole from Olivia had not been ruined from the running. Rain dripped down her face and into her clothes beneath her coat.

From under the hood of the jacket, Therese could barely hear or see anything but rain. She got nervous that she might miss the Long Road and simply stay on the highway forever. What if a driver came along and hit her because he could not see her through the downpour? That would get Amy and Jeff's attention. Maybe she should not have made the choice to leave. Her nose ran and mixed with the water on her face. Her ears rang and started to sting from the blood rushing through them. She heard a real ringing and she realized there was something coming up behind her. She turned around and saw it was a bicycle. Someone rang the bell, over and over. Therese jumped off the road and tried to run into the bush, but it was impossible for her to hide from the man. She was wearing a bright yellow rain jacket. She was probably the only visible thing in the storm. Therese stopped and turned to face the man approaching on the bicycle. If he was a bad man, he would rape her. He would kill her. She would not see Mama or Felix or Virgil again. She would not see Robert. Therese clapped her hands once and opened them to Heaven. *God, it is up to you.* The machine gun the man had slung over his shoulder was very large, and she could see it long before she could see the man's face. Then she realized it was Kisungu, the guard from Olivia's house. He made a noise with his mouth that sounded like he was gasping for breath, only louder. He was laughing at her. Therese planted her fists on her hips and waited for him to come closer.

"Get on," he told her, once he stopped. She glared at him, but then she climbed onto his seat, and he stood up on the pedals and pumped them in the direction they came from. While he drove her home, he lectured her about how dangerous it was on the road. He told her that if she promised she would never run away again, he would not tell Olivia, who was fond of making girls who misbehaved clean the outhouse. Therese promised.

"Did Mwamini tell you I ran away?" she asked him. He said no, he saw Therese leave himself. She asked him why he did not come get her earlier. He told her he was waiting for her to turn back, but she never did.

CHAPTER THIRTEEN

T he storm continued for days. As angry as she was to be back, Therese was glad to have a dry place to sleep. The outhouse at Olivia's home was very traditional, and when she went to use it in the rain, her feet slipped around in the mud. She held the grab-bar and steadied herself over the hole as water dripped on the back of her neck. If the outhouse leaked, it was still not as bad as a bedroom leaking. It was not as bad as being out in the storm again. "I am lucky," Therese told herself.

The mood at Brianna's Village was very poor. The corn that they planted got too much rain and was ruined for the harvest. Supplies from The City were delayed because the road was washed out.

Therese had not seen Felix or Virgil for three days. She missed Robert. Because of the rain, she was sure the express boat had not left, but still she felt like a caged animal. She had been drawing water for Olivia, and her back was always sore. She had a cramping like an upset stomach that moved from her low belly to her back. Therese used the pit toilet, and a new smell hit her. It was metallic like rain and rich like butter. Her first period. She did not know what to do and then remembered the folded strips of fabric that had been placed on her mattress on her first day with Olivia. Therese sloshed through the mud back to her room. She felt swollen between her legs, and her whole body was sweaty. She made a little ball out of the fabric and tucked it into her underwear. Olivia walked in and lifted her chin at Therese.

"You've become a woman today?" she asked. Therese was nervous about that smell and now she was ashamed, but Olivia was the closest thing she had to a mama, and Therese didn't know who else she could talk to, so she said yes, she'd gotten her first period, and Olivia smiled.

"Congratulations. And be careful!" she warned. "Even though you feel like a child, everyone will think you're an adult. You'll have to behave like one now."

Therese thought Olivia would tell her something else, but instead, she unlocked the small suitcase next to her bed. Inside, Therese saw pink and blue boxes. Olivia hunched over the suitcase, blocking her view. When she turned around, she held out a small, plastic package to Therese. She opened it and found what she learned was a maxi pad. Olivia showed her how it worked and told her it was their secret. Therese would need to throw it away when nobody else was watching. That was the one Western gift, aside from money, that Olivia accepted from Brianna each month. Everyone else at the village used old fabric and had to wash it in the river, but Olivia had her special supplies. And now Therese did too.

Brianna finally made it back to the village. The storm had cleared, and the road was once again passable. She brought more gifts for the girls—new rain gear and boots. Even though the sun was finally shining, Therese ran back to her room to put them on. Her feet felt funny inside closed shoes, and the wellies rubbed against her shins, but getting around was so much easier! She walked through the mud to the listening lean-to, where Mwamini, Baby Giselle, Hiroute, Olivia, and Brianna waited for her. Their donor held Giselle on her lap and gave her a bottle.

"Will you translate, Therese?" Brianna asked. Therese nodded. Brianna said that she had been in contact with the woman who ran New Beginnings, the school on the other side of The City's Lake, and while the buildings were not completely finished, the next class was being assembled. She wanted to sponsor them all to participate in the training for six months. Mwamini and Hiroute hugged each other and squealed in happiness.

"Miss Brianna, when will we go?" Therese asked.

"I know you're in a hurry to get across the lake, Therese. I talked to Amy, and she told me about your news. I'm going over on the express boat the day after tomorrow. You and the other girls can come with me, but you have to ask FCS if it's okay first."

Therese hugged her and the girls and pulled Olivia up from her seat. She begged Olivia to make the call to FCS for her on her cell phone, and she had no choice because Brianna was watching. Because no other adult was there to take care of Therese's business, she had to do it herself. She grabbed Olivia's phone and told Amy that she would go across the lake with Brianna and that if she and Jeff wanted to come with her, she would be happy to work on the film with them. Amy was not in a position to argue. If Brianna was paying Therese's way, she didn't really need their permission. Amy agreed, and Brianna and Therese made plans to meet the crew in two days.

Olivia was thrilled that Therese was going to New Beginnings. It meant one less mouth to feed. She would even come on the ferry to take the girls across the lake. There was just one problem: Where would Felix and Virgil go once their stay at the hospital was over? Dr. Bingi would never let them be there for the whole time Therese was gone, and without her living at Brianna's Village, they wouldn't be allowed to live there either. Then Therese thought about how Robert had been working with FCS to get what he needed—publicity, money, an education. If Therese could give all the money she made with FCS to a responsible adult, they could make sure the boys went to school and had a safe place to stay. The only person Therese could think of to take care of two young boys was Mr. Muhangi. Before she hung up with Amy, she asked her if Thomas would take her to see him on the way to the dock. She also asked for some time with Felix and Virgil before she left. Amy agreed and said she would see her soon.

For the rest of the day, Therese spent her time putting together plans for her brother and Virgil. She also packed up her small bundle of belongings. She fished out her journal and put it on the top of the pile. She wanted to share it with Brianna. She was the only English-speaking person she knew who had not seen the footage from FCS's film, and she wanted to know what Brianna thought about how she told her story. Mwamini and Hiroute packed up their secondhand clothes, while Olivia was busy putting other people in charge of various tasks for the next few days. It was the first time she had been away from the compound for more than a day. Therese told her about her plan for Felix and Virgil, and Olivia used her cell phone to withdraw the money from the bank that Therese would give to Mr. Muhangi. The whole village was buzzing like a beehive around the news of their journey.

At night Therese could not sleep. She thought about what she would find on the other side of the lake. Would it be a big city? What would the port look like? The General had crossed the lake. Where was he? What would life be like for the women he had dragged along, and was Mama there with him? What about Felix and Virgil? Would they be safe at the church with Mr. Muhangi? How long before they were released from the hospital? Where would Robert be in six months? Would Therese ever see him again? She had so many questions and wrote them down as a prayer to God. *Please help me find the answers. Please help me find my way.* She sweated in bed and felt the strange, squeezy feeling in her lower belly. Therese listened to the rumble of Olivia's snoring. For someone who took care of so many, she seemed not to worry at all.

In the morning, after breakfast, two trucks arrived. One was Brianna's SUV with the gun and the slash through it. The other was the FCS Jeep. Thomas waved at Therese through the windshield. The women at Brianna's Village all sang, "Go well, friends. Go well, friends." They said their goodbyes as though it would be forever. Olivia, Hiroute, Mwamini, and Giselle got into Brianna's truck. She had arranged to have a special car seat just for Giselle, but the baby cried and cried until Mwamini agreed to hold her on her lap. Therese got into the FCS truck with the crew. The village's children chased them partway down the highway until their muddy tire tracks became invisible and blended into the black of the pavement.

Mr. Muhangi would go with the crew and Therese to the hospital to visit Felix and Virgil. He wanted to see them before they were released to him. When they went to pick him up, Therese noticed that he had made two neat, little nests for the boys in the corner next to his own, like a mother bird. She thought they would be very happy there, Therese told him. She also noticed that Mr. Muhangi had on his special church clothes. That must be for the trip into The City.

"You look very nice," Therese told him. He took the job of caring for her brother and unbrother seriously, she thought. She was glad she could provide some payment for him. On the way to The City, Mr. Muhangi noticed the village that was newly burned, and he gasped. Therese was glad that The General's group moved across the lake and away from where her loved ones would be living. Mr. Muhangi asked her if she was worried about meeting The General on the other side of the water, but Therese was done being afraid. She told him as long as her family was safe, she was not scared. He took her hand and kissed it. He did not ask about Mama.

Virgil was in the recovery room. Dr. Bingi had put a pin into his leg so that it would grow the right way. He lay in a bed with his cast up in a sling that hung from the ceiling. Desanges fed him ginger ale through a straw, and he looked like the happiest boy alive. Felix sat on the other side, nervously pulling what was left of his eyebrow. The second Mr. Muhangi was through the door, he high-fived Virgil and scooped up Felix in his arms. They both started weeping, and Therese knew everything would be okay. She could not tell the boys goodbye. It was just too hard to know she would be leaving them, even for six months. Therese watched the reunion between Mr. Muhangi and the boys and that was enough for her.

Robert had promised to visit Felix that day, but Jeff told Therese that his sponsor for high school had come into town, and he would probably not be able to see her off. She was happy to hear that Robert would go to school, but she was crushed that she would not be able to tell him goodbye. The whole time in the hospital, Jeff filmed the action in Virgil's room. It felt a little like a party. Felix was busy admiring Amy's bright orange hair, so Jeff turned the camera on Therese. He asked, "How do you feel about Mr. Muhangi watching after them for a while?"

"Aside from me, I think he is the only one who really knows them, and as long as there are no parents around, I feel like he is the best person," she said. Instead of really thinking about what all of that meant, Therese was thinking about Robert. How could he let her go like that without coming by? Did he know how she felt about him? She told herself that the next time she saw him she would admit everything.

"Therese? Therese?" said Amy. She had been asking her questions, but Therese had not heard her. Therese said, "I do not want to be on camera."

"Do you want to shoot a bit?" asked Jeff. She took the camera from him. She shot Felix showing Mr. Muhangi the splint on his hand and telling him how The Mole broke his fingers with a hammer. Felix went into great detail about how each finger was broken for a person he refused to kill. He told the story about how he saved his own life by writing speeches in English and French for The General. It was more than he had told Therese or Dr. Bingi in group meeting. Therese loved that Felix was able to talk to Mr. Muhangi. Virgil interrupted by bragging about the fall from the climbing structure. He had never had a problem talking. Therese looked to Jeff for direction. He whispered, "I'll get the rest of the story later."

—⧣—

It was time to meet Brianna at the dock. They packed up the equipment and Therese said a quick goodbye to the boys and Mr. Muhangi. She could not manage any more than that. Thomas took them on a short drive to the middle of downtown, where the dock was. Fortunately it was a dry day. She could not believe the size of the marina. Boats of all sizes were parked against the pier. Huge ships were tied up next to tiny fishing boats and larger cargo boats. It was chaotic, and Therese had the feeling of something about to happen. A smell of fish hit her nose, and she wondered which fishing boat was responsible for the strong scent. Vendors selling everything from pineapples to suitcases walked the length of the boardwalk.

They unloaded the truck and carried their bags and equipment to where Andrew waved from a grassy area set back from the water. Under a large tarp, Brianna, Olivia, Mwamini, Giselle, and Hiroute relaxed in plastic chairs with cold drinks. A stooped, old man handed tickets to them and collected money from Brianna. Beside them under the tarp was a group of about twelve others. A small boat called the Marine Express bobbed in the water. Surely that could not be their boat. Therese counted the people in the group. They were eight, including baby Giselle. Were they all going on that boat with the locals? Andrew gave Therese a Coke. The bottle, wet and smooth, almost slipped from her hand. The hot, still air made her so grateful just to hold the cool, unopened bottle. The old man collected suitcases from all the passengers, tagged them with some chalk, and stacked them in a pile near the pier. A younger man in a captain's uniform dropped the luggage into a cargo compartment in the front of the boat. The passengers stood around for what seemed like forever, and finally, it was time to board. The locals got on first. Therese's group said goodbye to Andrew and then to Thomas, who were headed back to the hospital to drive Mr. Muhangi home. Therese turned to the boat, which seemed to sink lower and lower as each person embarked. The stooped old man climbed onto it and offered his hand to people crossing from the pier. Therese looked back at the port and saw a familiar form. It was Robert! He moved like a wobbly human tripod through the busy scene. He struggled across the wet grass to where they were boarding. Therese ran to him and they met right where the grass contacted the pier. He dropped his cane and put his arms around her. All his weight leaned against Therese. He hugged her to his chest. His heart drummed hard and fast, and Therese could feel it pounding through her all the way into her back.

He kissed her, hard on the mouth. She could smell a dusty cigarette lingering on his breath. Her lips had felt dry in the hot air, but they felt soft against Robert's. It was the first time anyone had kissed Therese on the mouth. She did not know quite what to do so she kissed him back. Therese was surprised when he opened his mouth and put his tongue on hers. She giggled and pushed her tongue back against his. She opened her eyes, and his were closed. Therese pulled back from his mouth, and they held each other like that for what seemed like a long time.

"I don't want to leave you," she whispered into his chest.

"I'll be here when you get back," he said. She imagined him in The City without her or Jeff or Amy. How long could a one-legged boy get by in The City? Therese looked toward the Marine Express. People were tightly crammed into the cabin. Suddenly she did not want to get on the boat. Jeff called to her through a window.

"Let's go, Therese!"

She gave Robert his cane and ran to the boat. Waving goodbye, she packed herself into the cabin. The young captain started up the engine, and it made a terrible coughing sound. They pushed away from the dock. Therese squeezed in next to Jeff, who had to sit sideways in the seat. Somewhere up front were Brianna and the other girls from the village. She could hear Giselle crying as the fumes from the engine seeped through the windows. It seemed like there were twice as many people as there should be in there. She strained to see the front of the boat, but it was too crowded inside. The smell of sweaty bodies filled the cabin. Amy turned around from the seat in front of her and smiled at her. She held up the Coke, which she must have left at the dock when she ran to Robert. She took it from Amy and opened it. Therese was a bit sick to her stomach from the fumes, so she took a sip and felt better. Water spilled over the edge of the boat, and spray from the lake came through the window. The coughing engine made her a little nervous. *What lived in this huge lake besides crocodiles?* she wondered.

"Welcome to the express boat," said Jeff, blowing a bubble and snapping his gum.

"How long until we get there?" Therese asked. She strained to look out the window at Robert, but Jeff's head was in the way. He was busy adjusting his camera.

"About three hours, if we're lucky," he said, opening his window a bit more. She tried to settle her stomach by taking small sips of the Coke. From the front of the boat, Giselle cried hysterically. She sobbed in hiccups and gasps. Therese wanted to cry too but kept herself busy with her Coke. The sugar in it made her heart race and it left a film on her tongue. She thought about the last thing her mouth had touched. She missed Robert already and wondered if Jeff was rewinding footage of her kissing Robert. The thought only made her feel sicker.

Across the aisle was a large, brown woman who wore Western clothing. She had her eyes closed and fanned herself with a fashion magazine with English on its cover. She wondered where the brown woman came from. It was almost as if she could read

Therese's mind because with her eyes still closed, she said in English, "I've been on this boat a dozen times, and six times it broke down."

"Why do you take it then?" Therese asked.

"It's still faster than the slow boat. That can take days," she said. Therese was happy for the distraction. Suddenly the left engine went silent and smoke came from that side of the boat. The captain slowed down, opened a hatch in front, and climbed out with an extinguisher. Everyone who had not opened a window quickly did. When they were stopped, the smell of the people and the fumes from the working engine made everyone feel sick. The sun beat down on the boat and Therese was miserable in the heat. She finished her Coke and instantly wanted another. Giselle was finally quiet. She must have gotten tired from crying and fallen asleep.

"See what I mean?" said the brown woman across the aisle. The young captain talked into a cell phone outside. Therese peered beyond him and saw only the lake. She strained to see out other people's windows but could see only water. Sweat beaded on her forehead and ran down her face. The rocking of the boat had the Coke in her tummy sloshing around. Amy pulled out her phone and stuck it under her massive hair. Who was she calling from the middle of the lake?

"You tell him we need a boat right now. And if he doesn't send it immediately, we're going public with the story. Associated Press, the UN, the works," she said. Jeff patted her on the shoulder and gave her a thumbs-up. Therese saw the young captain balancing on the side of the boat with the extinguisher in one hand and his cell phone in the other. He walked to the front and climbed back in through the window. He turned the boat slightly, and they were moving again, only much more slowly. The people in the front of the boat near the captain started talking about what was going on. Amy turned to her.

"We lost an engine, and now the captain's worried the working one will blow too. We'll be stuck in the middle of the lake, if he doesn't pull onto an island," she said.

Therese was grateful for the opportunity to get off the boat but nervous about where they would land. Were the bad men there? The little boat took another hour to labor its way to a small island. Out the window across the aisle, she could see the beach. There was no dock to land on, so the captain pulled in as close as he could to the sand. Because Therese was at the back, she was the first to get out. She stepped into the sunshine and made her way to the front of the boat. The nose of the Marine Express was about twelve feet from the water line on the beach. She was surprised to see the stooped old man from the pier at the bow. He took her hand and gestured to the beach. She hiked up her wrap and jumped into the clear water.

CHAPTER FOURTEEN

I t seemed that the entire island village came to see their arrival. About fifty people, mostly women and children, gathered around Therese. She turned to catch her small, plastic bag of collected treasures as the old man threw it to her. Instantly she was mobbed by the children.

"Money! Money! Money!" they cried, in English. There must have been a hotel on the island, if they could speak English. As the others on the boat came onshore, they were also mobbed. They all clutched their belongings tightly. If the children knew the contents of Therese's bag were worthless to them, they would have left her alone. The crowd fell silent for a moment, as Amy, Brianna, and Jeff jumped from the boat and walked through the shallow water. The children left Therese alone, immediately drawn by the strange-looking white people. Some of the smaller kids grabbed their *mzungu* hands and pulled them onto the shady porch of a small shack on the beach. Jeff saw this as a great opportunity to get some footage, but one little boy spotted the gum in his mouth. Within seconds, all the children swarmed around him, crying, "Candy! Candy! Candy!"

As Therese expected, Amy's hair got some attention too. The little girls strained to touch it and pat her head. Brianna pulled out a digital camera to shoot the chaos. She took pictures of the children and showed them images of themselves. Therese thought about the first time she saw herself on camera. Compared to those children, she was an expert on being photographed. All the other passengers from The City sat around on the beach. A tired island woman with a huge basket of bananas wove through the crowd. Everyone from the boat was too hot, or too seasick to eat, but the local children followed her movements hungrily. Before Therese could suggest it, Brianna approached her. She took Therese's hand and led her to the lady with the bananas. Jeff and Amy left their fans and followed her with the microphone and camera.

"*Jambo sana*," the banana seller said in a tired voice.

"How much for all these bananas?" Brianna asked, and Therese translated.

"Twenty dollars?" the lady asked, unsure of herself. Even if English-speaking tourists often visited there, she had probably never sold a whole basket at once. Therese nodded and translated back. Brianna pulled out the money and gave it to the banana lady. She looked as if she had a treasure in her hand and she pulled Brianna in for a big hug. Brianna handed out fruit to all the locals on the beach. The children crowded around her and sang their thank-yous.

"How long since that little guy last ate?" Jeff asked, pointing at a toddler with a runny nose and a giant belly. Therese asked his mama, who peeled a banana for him. She said three days, and Therese translated for Jeff. She thought about how unlucky they were to have a boat that broke down in the middle of the lake, and about how their bad luck became the good fortune of the villagers. She watched how happy the people were to have one tiny banana. A little girl with a terrible cough came over, chewing her piece of fruit. She took Therese's hand. Therese looked into her huge eyes. That was the life that the little girl knew—sickness, hunger, isolation.

"The only difference between her and me is where we were born," Brianna said, pointing at the banana lady. Therese felt fortunate to have Brianna in her life. She was generous in a way Therese had never seen before. As they sat side by side on the sandy beach, Brianna explained that everyone in America got an education.

Even girls. That did not mean that everyone in America would be rich and lucky, like Brianna, but it meant that most would not grow up to be poor banana-sellers with too many sick children. When Therese heard about America, she wondered what it would be like to go to school in such a place. But then she thought about Mama, and she felt guilty for wanting to be anywhere other than looking for her. Her thoughts were interrupted when a gleaming, two-decker boat buzzed across the lake in their direction. Everyone on the beach turned at the sound of the giant engines.

"Here's our ride!" announced Amy. The boat had a government seal on its side. There were smartly dressed crew members onboard, and they all carried large, automatic weapons on their hips. Therese wondered how Amy was able to call in the favor from the Congolese government. The boat dropped a large anchor, and one of the crew leaned a gangplank off the doorway. Amy and Jeff hurried to the boat so they could record everyone getting on. Therese stepped onto the deck and watched the villagers eat their fruit. They waved goodbye to her. She saw the sick-looking toddler with his mama on the beach and looked at baby Giselle with Mwamini on the boat. She also held a banana. The difference between them was that she was going to a place of opportunities with her mama. She was going to New Beginnings.

The ride on the government boat was short. Therese did not realize how fast they could cross the lake with the proper transportation. She sat on the top deck with her friends. The air was fresh and clean, and she hardly noticed the rocking of the boat. As they slowed to the marina at Port Town, she looked at the settlement. It was much smaller than The City, but it was interesting. Even though it was a port, big lush trees dotted the waterfront. People on the boardwalk looked busy and happy. Therese felt a pang of sadness at leaving Robert, Mr. Muhangi, Virgil, and Felix behind, but she also felt the pull and the excitement of what was to come.

CHAPTER FIFTEEN

Therese had been at New Beginnings for a few weeks, and it was quite different from Brianna's Village. It was huge, like its own city. The campus sat in a valley, surrounded by several small towns. The women from neighboring villages built the place with their own hands. The structures were made from brick and had poured-concrete floors. The windows were glass, and the roofs were blue. The low-lying lawn in the middle of the campus was soggy, like a marsh. Spindly, staked fruit trees lined the walkways and promised nourishment for future students. A new vegetable garden boasted *beans, peas, lettuce* on little flags in the ground. Everything was brand new. There was electricity and running water.

Women from nearby areas stood in line every day to ask questions about how to register for the next class. Therese felt lucky to have a sponsor like Brianna to help her get into the program. She suggested that Therese become a mentor for New Beginnings. She taught English and French classes to girls and women much older than she was, and the program's director, a tall, beautiful Congolese woman named Marie, said Therese was more than qualified. Her days were full, teaching classes, and she was happy. Therese was also learning how to use a computer to communicate, and how to use a sewing machine, so she could make clothing, purses, and wall hangings to sell in the gift shop. She was taking a special class on how to defend herself from any potential attacker. She went to group meetings and massage therapy every day. Compared to hauling cassava at Brianna's Village, this was like a vacation.

She shared a bright room with Mwamini and baby Giselle in a dormitory building that held several other apartments, including the one that Hiroute and Esther shared. The first day she arrived, Therese was surprised for a moment to see Esther there, but then she remembered that Dr. Bingi and Desanges helped her with her application months ago, before Therese left the hospital. She was also shocked not to see Esther's owl-eyed baby boy. The infant, who still had no name by the time Therese left the hospital, died in his sleep a few weeks earlier. His mother did not seem sad, maybe because the baby was put inside her by a bad man. Therese often tried to strike up conversations with Esther, but she stared at Therese through her one eye and made her uneasy.

The FCS crew stayed in a hotel near New Beginnings. There was no news of The General, but Therese told herself that she could feel Mama close by. With no word of the militia, Amy had some spare time when Therese arrived. She and Olivia helped her get settled into her new room, but then they left. Once Brianna had delivered Hiroute, Mwamini, Giselle, and Therese to New Beginnings, she went home to her family in America. Therese hoped Brianna and Amy would not forget about her.

Jeff had given Therese a small video camera of her own, so that she could film her experience at New Beginnings. She recorded herself and sent videos to Felix in the hospital. Now that she could type on a computer and send e-mail, Therese could also write to him. Dr. Bingi promised to help Mr. Muhangi transition Felix and Virgil from the hospital to the church on the Long Road. Thinking of them made her feel homesick, so she concentrated on Mama instead.

—ɯ—

In group therapy, Hiroute did not look so good. Her cough sounded like a barking dog. She hacked into a rag, and it was almost always bloody. She stopped going to classes. Therese feared that Hiroute was dying and the reason Brianna sponsored her was to let her live out her remaining days in a place that was more comfortable than Olivia's home.

"Will you get some water or something?" demanded Mwamini, irritated at Hiroute's coughing.

Mwamini tried to get on camera every time Therese recorded poor Hiroute. Giselle was like Therese's baby sister, and she found that if given the choice to shoot her or her selfish mother, she always chose Giselle. Their room was a bit crowded, with Mwamini, Giselle, and Therese. Mwamini never missed a chance to complain.

"It sure is getting tight in here," Mwamini said. As if Esther parroted Mwamini, she came in rubbing her own back and complaining, "Hiroute's coughing kept me up most of the night."

They had to agree with her. The coughing woke Giselle, and she'd been grumpy all day.

"I'm tired of being kept up all night. Hiroute should go to Heaven and take care of all of the unwanted babies," said Esther. Mwamini and Esther's attitudes were the only unpleasant things there.

Therese started to make her first wall hanging in sewing. She planned to embroider a picture of a mother pig and her two babies. If it was good enough, she could sell it at the crafts center. Her fingers did not like the sewing machine, and when she ran the needle through the fabric, the whole thing got all bunched up.

"You're terrible at crafts," said Mwamini. "You'll never be able to support your family if you don't learn to sew."

"I'm not here just to learn to sew, Mwamini. I want more," Therese told her again. Mwamini snorted and turned away, but Therese got her revenge. Mwamini was in her English class and was the worst student. The English classes were going better than the wall hanging, as most of the women and girls Therese taught could already read and write a little in Swahili. The ones, like Mwamini, who did not read in their native tongue, didn't catch on as quickly. Mwamini's learning was much like Therese's wall hanging, all bunched up.

She received an e-mail from Felix, and he sounded much like his regular self. He must have been learning on the computer at the hospital. He reported that he and Virgil played soccer every day against Stuttering Eric and his cousin. He also sent a picture of himself. He had more hair, and it looked like he was not pulling at it so much anymore. He was waving in the photo, and the splint was still on his finger, but he said it would come off in a few days. The more the boys healed, the more anxious they were to be with Mr. Muhangi. That little red boat and a fishing pole were just waiting for them.

Amy and Jeff finally came by with some news about The General. He fled the area in an airplane. Therese could not picture where the nearest airport was; he must have had a landing strip nearby. The FCS crew had no news about the slaves he was dragging along with him, but they continued to look for survivors. Therese was nervous that Mama was in his ranks and he killed them all off, but she kept telling herself what Brianna said: "No news is good news."

Brianna agreed to help pay to send Virgil and Felix to a private boys' school in a nearby village, once they were settled in with Mr. Muhangi. Therese often thought about all the wonderful people she had met since her village was attacked. Brianna helped her so much, more than any other person. She sometimes sat on the front stoop of her dorm and thought about what lay beyond the borders of her country. Danger? Education? Freedom? Brianna came from a place so far away that Therese could not even imagine it.

Of course she daydreamed about Robert a lot. When she went back to The City, would he be waiting for her? Her thoughts drifted from him to Mama, to Virgil, to Felix, and back, and then it was time to take a class or teach one. Her favorite activity was chorus.

It reminded her of growing up and singing in church choir with
the boys and girls from her village. The music room was small, and
the voices were all women's, but the songs were just as beautiful.
Life was sweet there, but it was only temporary.

—◊—

Therese was singing with the New Beginnings choir in the
music room when Amy burst through the door. The teacher, a
woman from Kinshasa, looked irritated by the interruption, until
she saw Amy's face. The singing stopped, and Therese was sure she
would tell her that Hiroute died. Instead she ran up and whispered
in her ear, "The Floating Hospital has found your mother, and she
is alive!"

Therese jumped from her riser and ran out the door with her.
She thought her heart might burst out of her chest. She sprinted
into the bright, harsh sunlight of the central lawn, leaped into
Amy's arms and cried happy tears into her red curls. Because they
did not allow men in New Beginnings, Amy led Therese to the
front gate, where Jeff was already rolling his camera on her. She
turned to his lens with tears running down her face and said,
"They found Mama."

Amy gave her the news right away. "The General left his slaves
to die on the side of a volcano near The City. Many were sick,
injured, or dying. Luckily a hospital that had been built on a ship
came floating by and picked up most of the women, and the men
who were with them. Only the women who were healthy enough
survived the long trip that brought them here." Therese said, "That's
good news. If Mama was able to make it this far, maybe she'll be
well for our reunion. Can I please go to meet the Floating Hospital
when it pulls into the marina?"

She could not wait to see the boat. Amy did not seem so sure.
She looked at her feet, avoiding Therese's eyes. Therese wondered
what was making Amy nervous.

"Therese, can I have your camera?" asked Jeff. "I need to start editing what you shot at New Beginnings."

Therese ran back to her room to get it, and as she passed Hiroute's room, she saw her lying in bed with her eyes closed. She looked very bad, and on Therese's way back to Jeff, she stopped by the New Beginnings medical clinic to tell someone about her.

"If there's anything you haven't told us in the last few weeks, you might want to share it now," said Jeff. Therese asked him what he meant.

"Once your mama's boat comes in, we'll contact you, and things are going to be exciting. We don't want to miss anything," Amy said. Therese thought of her journal, and how she'd been keeping a record of her life in it. She asked Amy if she wanted it.

"Hang onto it," said Amy. "You may want to keep writing about everything. Who knows? Maybe someone will want to publish it sometime." Therese thought about how reading books in English always made her feel connected to the people who wrote them. Would anyone outside Congo really be interested in her book? She felt that strange pull of a world outside of the walls of New Beginnings, and even beyond the borders of Congo. Jeff asked Therese if she would like to see the latest footage once it was edited.

"It depends if my story has a happy ending," she told him. As she said it, they all turned to see two women in *kangas* and face masks go into Hiroute's room carrying a stretcher. Moments later they emerged with Hiroute's sheet-covered body.

Before Hiroute was sent away to be buried, the choir sang a beautiful song for her in the chapel. Therese was so excited to see Mama that she could hardly concentrate on the task at hand. They sang about the birds and about souls going to Heaven, but all Therese could think about was how she was once somebody's baby. She could have been someone's mama someday. Therese thought about all the lives Hiroute touched: her parents', her friends', her husband's, and Therese's. She felt tired, thinking about what they had all been through in the previous six months, but she knew that she still had a family, and Mama was out there, waiting for her. Hiroute would be buried near her village on the other side of the lake. Therese hoped she still had a family there that would mourn for her.

—⟋⟍—

She was on her way back to the dorm with Mwamini and Giselle when Amy approached in a hurry. Mwamini stuck around, even though Amy did not have any equipment with her.

She told Therese that the hospital boat was on its way into the harbor. Jeff waited with an armed guard outside the front gate. When they exited the compound, the guard was shooing children away from Jeff. It seemed that every child in Port Town had heard that there was a white person with gum and expensive equipment nearby. Once they started walking, the crowd fell away. It was only a few blocks to the port. The road was muddy. Jeff and Amy had big hiking boots on. Therese was wearing her donated Wellies. She thought about the picture Mama would see when Therese approached her. She knew that she was taller and thinner than when Mama last saw her. Therese had changed into a young woman, but she thought Mama would be most shocked at her rain boots. She wiggled her toes inside. The cotton dress, given to Therese back at Olivia's home, felt suddenly a bit snug in the shoulders. Therese grinned thinking about Mama.

It was so hot and sticky that Amy's giant mane was plastered to the side of her face. Jeff walked a few paces behind them, trying to get a steady shot of Therese. As they approached the dock, she was astonished at the size of the Floating Hospital. The boat was as big as any government building that she had seen. Maybe bigger. It was white, with windows all around, and a helicopter on the top deck. There were dozens of people waving from the railings. Through the drizzle, Therese recognized a green head wrap in the crowd on the lower level. It was her mama. Therese was a bit surprised at how small and stooped over she looked, like a *nyanya*, a grandmother, with a cane. She looked as if she carried a heavy weight on her head, but there was no basket that Therese could see. Even from the shore, Therese could spot circles under her eyes. She looked tired and old, but she was standing up. She was not in a hospital bed, or worse, a ditch. Therese could not keep her feet on the ground and started jumping up and down.

"Everywhere I thought I saw her," she said to the camera. "In the lobby of the hospital, walking on the side of the road. But it was never her. That is Mama there!" Therese pointed at the boat where Mama stood, grinning. Mama wiped tears or rain from her cheek. If only Felix could be there too. They just found out about Mama the day before, and although Therese sent him an e-mail telling him the good news, there was not enough time to get him across the lake to be with them.

A gangplank was lowered onto the pier, and a little girl with her arm in a cast walked down, helped by a teenage boy and a kind-looking man. They looked exhausted, and they were holding each other up. Mama was one of the lucky ones who could walk by herself, but she grasped the handrail as if she felt she would fall over, and she was wearing a leg brace. She had a hospital bracelet on her wrist, and a friendly looking orderly cut it off and kissed her goodbye once she was on solid ground. Mama carried a small plastic bag, like Therese's. Fleetingly she wondered what was inside. They worked their way toward each other through the crowd, and the next thing Therese knew, she was wrapped in Mama's arms. In her dress, Mama's shoulders were bare, and Therese was shocked that she was tall enough to rest her head against Mama's neck. That was where she stayed for a long, long time, taking in her Mama-smell and her Mama-touch. People pushed past them, trying to get their loved ones home or to nearby hospitals. Therese and Mama did not move. They would never let each other go.

—⁂—

As they walked toward New Beginnings, Therese told Mama about the film Amy and Jeff were making. Because a camera was always with them, Mama spoke to her in English.

"What if The General sees this movie? Will we be in danger?" Mama asked.

"Telling your story is the way to keep us safe, Mama. The world will not let him get away with this," Therese said, taking her hand.

Mama described how she and Felix were taken by The General's men. They were separated almost immediately, as he was taken to become a soldier for The General or a miner for The Mole. Mama had no doubt that he was too small and good-hearted for the militia, and she prayed that his language skills would save him, especially if he was taken to the mines and forced into slavery.

Mama, with her stately beauty, had been taken as a concubine for The General, so she was almost always on the move with him. He dragged her through the bush, raping her whenever he pleased. His men raped her too. The General soon learned she had the gift of language, and from then on, she also managed his communications to the outside world, both in English and French. Mama said that was the only thing that kept her alive. When she could, she helped child soldiers write letters to their families. Therese asked her how she convinced someone to deliver the letters to The City. She shook her head and said, "The same way I got food and water." Therese did not have the heart to ask anything else.

Amy asked, "Luna, would you be willing to tell us more?"

"I need some time with my daughter. Later, perhaps," said Mama.

Arms around each other, Mama and Therese trudged through the mud and the drizzle to New Beginnings. The crowd of kids at the entrance met the crew again, swarming around Amy and Jeff as they said goodbye at the gate. The crew would come back the next day to help Mama plan for a reunion with Felix. Mama and Therese were escorted through the gate by the security guard to meet with the program's director.

Mama was impressed by Marie, who was easily six feet tall in her flip-flops. The director explained that since they were in the middle of the semester, and since there was a vacancy in the dorm, Mama was welcome to stay as long as she liked. "This place can be hard to understand," said Marie in Swahili. She smiled a wide, warm smile at Mama and reached across the table to take her hand. She said that she was a rape survivor too, but the bad things that happened to her did not define her life. She had become the director of a very powerful organization and had used her experience to move her life forward. Therese thought about the book she was writing in her journal, and about the film she was making with Amy and Jeff. She hoped they would show the world what had happened in Congo and help make sure it never happened again.

Mama nodded as Marie spoke gently to her, but she said nothing at first. She looked around the bright office as sunlight broke through the clouds and streamed onto the desk. A large flowering plant was perched on a corner table, and an overhead photograph of New Beginnings hung on the wall. Beyond the windows, Mama could see solar panels all over the roofs of the buildings. Her eyebrows pulled together with a question.

"Where's the generator?" she asked, pointing to overhead light. Therese remembered how, when she first went to the hospital in The City, she did not know where the lights came from. She kept looking around for generators until the Blue Head man explained electricity.

"We generate our own power here," said Marie.

—ᴍ—

Therese spent most of the afternoon showing Mama around. She could not believe how beautiful the campus was, and the running water and electricity were exciting to her. Mwamini and Giselle moved into Esther's room so that Mama and Therese could be together. It would be the first time in six months other than on the Floating Hospital that Mama had slept in a bed. That evening, as they got ready to go to sleep, Mama emptied out her plastic bag onto her pillow. Therese was surprised that she had only medicine and a mosquito net inside.

"Mama, did the bad men make you sick?" Therese asked. Mama looked down at the stash of pills and nodded. Therese was instantly nervous that Mama would die the way Hiroute did.

"The bad men and the mosquitoes. I'm being treated for malaria too," Mama said. Therese read the bottles, but most of them had names she could not pronounce. "I had no mosquito net until the Floating Hospital gave me one. The mosquitoes can kill you as easily as the bad men. The difference is that the mosquito's bite itches for a few days, gives you a fever and chills, and then makes your stomach empty out. What the bad man puts in you can make your belly fill up, and it hurts forever."

"I know, Mama," Therese said. Mama opened her arms to her, and she stepped in. Mama closed her in a long embrace, and Therese inhaled her through her nose, her mouth, and her skin. Mama removed her head wrap, and Therese was shocked that her hair had turned almost completely white. When she was taken from Therese, her hair was in tiny braids and was black as the night. Now, she had longer, knotty-looking dreadlocks, but they were white. Mama was so young, about thirty-two, if Therese remembered right. How could her hair be that color, she asked, her fingers winding themselves through Mama's hair.

"I grew a grey hair every day I was away from you and Felix," she said, crying.

Her tears fell onto Therese's neck when she hugged her again.

For the next few days, Mama was always with her. Wearing donated clothes from New Beginnings, she sat in on the classes Therese taught. She sang in the choir with Therese, and she went to group therapy. Her sewing was much better than Therese's, and she finished the pig wall hanging for her. She even held Giselle when Mwamini and Therese went to self-defense class. Mama was so involved in Therese's life that Therese hardly noticed at first that she was growing restless. She kept her medicine in her plastic bag with her mosquito net, and she always stripped her bed each morning, as if she were planning to leave. Marie told Mama that she was welcome to stay, but Therese began to see she had other plans. One day, when she was in the gift shop with Therese, she looked at the wall hanging that Therese started and she completed. She pointed at one of the piglets and said, "My other baby is out there, Therese. I need to see Felix." And Therese knew she would be going soon. Therese could not blame her. Therese felt the same way Mama did when she was looking for her.

"I need to get treatment at a proper hospital to fix my knee. I need my life back," she said, and Therese could not argue.

Amy came each day with news from The City. She told her about Robert and how he was doing since he was back in school. Therese ached to be near him, but she knew New Beginnings was helping to heal and educate her in a way he could not. She was determined to get through the final months of her education, even if it meant saying goodbye to Mama for a little while.

One day, when Amy brought a camera to record them, she told Mama that the slow boat to The City could take her across anytime she was ready. Felix and Virgil were already living with Mr. Muhangi, and they were waiting for her at their home in the church on the Long Road. Mama wasted no time. She had seen that Therese was alive and that she used Mama's gifts to keep herself safe. Mama promised to give Therese's family hugs and kisses from her.

The next day, she was gone.

—◊◊◊—

Several weeks later, Therese graduated from New Beginnings. She was honored by Marie, who chose her to make a speech at commencement. In her graduating class were Mwamini and Esther. In the audience were Brianna, Olivia, Amy, Jeff, Mama, Mr. Muhangi, Virgil, Felix, and Robert. It was the first time she had seen boys and men at New Beginnings. She felt as if all those people had been on a very long journey with her. Therese spoke about what happened in the village and how they got there. She stood before a large crowd and said there was no reason that Congolese girls should not enjoy the same peace and education that other girls around the world did. After Marie handed her certificate to her, Therese sang and danced with her family. The truth was that her future was very uncertain and confusing. She wanted to continue her education. She wanted to be with Robert. She wanted to go back home and live on the Long Road with her family. She wanted to see Brianna's home across the ocean. Wanting all these things was scary, and only God knew what would come next.

After the celebration died down, Brianna went to her with good news. She and Amy had spread the word about the Free Child Slaves film they made. Even though the movie was not edited, Jeff created what was called a trailer, and a company in Canada had shown an interest in distributing the completed film. Soon her story might be in movie theaters around the world. The film even had a name: *Unnatural Resources.*

Therese loved the title. It referred to many things, all the surprising gifts that helped her survive. To the English that Mama gave to her children. To the friendship between Brianna and Therese. To their power to live, and to create love with others, even when bad men tried to take everything away.

Then Brianna asked about the journal Therese had been writing. She said that it might help get the film a wider release if her story was also told in print. She ran back to her room and pulled out the plastic bag in which she kept her belongings. She fished out the journal and ran back to the hall where the graduation celebration was still going on. Without a word, she gave the journal to Brianna. Therese felt like she was putting her future in Brianna's hands.

"Maybe someday you can come visit us in California," said Brianna.

"I would like that," Therese said, grinning, wondering if it would ever happen.

PART TWO

Luna

CHAPTER SIXTEEN

Luna looks beyond the growing stalks of manioc and it feels like moments ago that her children were taken from her. The roots are so strong in fertile soil because The Volcano poured hot fury on this land. Luna has learned there is fortune in calamity. Had The Volcano not emptied all over the bad people who uprooted her from her children, she probably would not be sitting here today. She would not enjoy the sun on her face, the wisps of smoke drifting from the high peak, the cool, fresh breeze. She would not be watching her children's children play the treasure hunt game that children have played now for generations. *Thank you, friend volcano, for saving our lives,* she thinks.

Watching over these kids is joyful. The grandchildren love each other. Felix's boys and Therese's son and daughter give Virgil a run for his money; he helps Luna with them when their parents are busy at work. Felix teaches at the school on the Long Road, just as his father once did. Therese is a lawyer in The City, fighting for land rights for women.

"Are you ready, Mama?" Therese asks. She's been fiddling with the video camera to get it just right. Luna giggles. She never wanted to be in the limelight, but the old fears that The General would see the film and track her down have long receded. She wants to tell her story and make her daughter proud.

"How did you know the lake would become so valuable and lead to such exploitation?" Therese prompts.

"For many years, our people have talked about the giant fish making bubbles at the bottom of the lake. If you get close enough to it, you can see the bubbles from the shore. Children are told by their parents to fish with a short line. If you get greedy and drop a fishing line that's too long, the fish can swallow you up whole."

Therese hesitates. She has filmed hundreds of victims' stories. The tales have won women their land rights in court and helped to convict the men who abused them.

Luna smiles. "It's a good fairy tale. But now it's time for you to hear my story."

The film begins to roll.

—⟋⟋⟍—

On the day I was taken, Jean-Paul, my husband, and Alexandre, Justine's husband, were home with Therese and the boys. They had returned in time for us to leave the children with them and deliver the cassava and bananas to the market. It was late in the day, not my favorite time to go. The road can be dangerous after dark, and if we dallied, we would be forced to spend the night with our friend, Penda, in town, rather than risk the night walk home. Then in the morning, Jean-Paul would have to get the kids ready for Sunday school, and remind Therese over and over to put the water to boil early enough. He hated those tasks. No, we would not spend the night.

Justine, Virgil's mama, always went with me to the market. She had been setting up her bananas next to my cassava flour for as long as I could remember. The sound of the weavers accompanied us on our long walk.

The market was busy, and we'd gotten a late start. Customers were admiring Justine's bananas before she even set down her load. I unrolled my blanket next to hers and set down the flour. Ignoring the gathering crowd, she gave me a quick massage on my head and neck, as my basket was heavy, and we had been walking a great distance. She always was so loving, and she and I had raised our children together. I still miss her when I talk about her. I recall the last thing she said to me.

"Do you remember when we used to have to walk on the highway, each of us with a basket on our head, while nursing our boys? I'm so glad it's only the basket now."

I did not even notice the men hiding behind us. I was enjoying my neck massage. My eyes were closed. It was too painful to describe what happened next, but she refused to let go of my shoulders, even when they knocked her teeth out. I could not forget the image of my best friend being dragged off into the woods.

—⚥—

When I was taken by the militia, The General quickly realized that beauty was not my asset. I told him I had learned English in high school, and he saw that he finally had a translator he could use. Me, I felt like nothing. When you defined yourself as a mother, and when you found yourself separated from your children, you were no longer anything.

The days became weeks, which became months, and every day, I tried harder and harder to remember things about my family. The way Jean-Paul's toes always tapped—on the ground, on the church floor, even on the bed, when he was at rest. Therese's eyebrows knitting together as she puzzled over how to conjugate the verb "to lend" in English. Felix tracing the veins in my hands, telling me I was soft.

Those of us who The General kidnapped had been moved many times. He took every opportunity he had to move and to increase his army of children. He had giant vehicles, and no matter where we were camped, there were always children arriving in the backs of the trucks, hanging off the sides, sitting on the bumpers, packed into and onto every surface. I noted that most of the boys did not seem unhappy to be in The General's trucks. I never really saw where he kept the boy soldiers. He housed them and the mamas away from each other.

There were many girls and women in camp. Depending on The General's mood, we were starved, raped, or beaten. Many of the assaults on us were committed by boy soldiers. I never looked them in the eye; I learned not to do that the first time. It was an invitation to a more severe beating. I considered myself lucky, as I always had a roof over my head. The General kept me with him most of the time. Many of the other women had to sleep outside in the elements. I saw them when it was time for us to wash. Once a week, we would be marched to the nearest river, but sometimes there was no soap, and there was never a way to dry ourselves. We usually had to towel off with our wraps and put them on wet. It got to the point that, when The General invaded a nearby town, I was relieved. It usually meant food and new, cleaner clothes for the rest of us.

One day, at washing time, I recognized someone I knew. It had been months since I had seen a familiar face. But there was my friend Penda. As we stripped off our wraps near the river, I noticed her, retching dry heaves. I stooped to help her, gazing quickly up at the armed guard as if to say, "Please."

He nodded and looked at me earnestly. I asked her if she was all right, and she surprised me by saying, "I don't need your help."

"Penda, it's me, Luna," I told her. She said she knew, but she did not want to attract the attention of the guards. If they discovered she was with child, who knew what they would do to her? She was right. The General did not find pregnant woman attractive or useful. I squeezed her arm once and walked away to wash in the river. It was the last time I saw her.

Some women might have found The General attractive. He was tall with teeth that gleamed like stars. His hands were delicate, almost like a woman's. There is something most women do not know about The General: he had, on his bottom, a heart-shaped, white birth mark that looked as if the brown had been removed from his skin. Right next to it was the same shaped birthmark, but twice the darkness of his skin. It is almost as if God had cut out an oval of color from one part of his bottom and laid it over the other part.

Most women who had been raped and tortured by him did not have the luxury of living long enough to notice his backside. After months of having sex with him, I started to play a game with myself. I imagined he was Jean-Paul. I could almost hear him whisper that he loved me after we lay together. In the aftermath of rape, I could almost feel Jean-Paul's toes wiggling under our blanket as The General snored. Jean-Paul never drank as much as my captor, but he snored too. Perhaps all men snored. I could not be sure, but the ones I had been with did.

Aside from my march to wash near the river, and the occasional break to relieve myself, I hardly left our tent. Unlike the other women in camp, I was not expected to cook, to clean latrine pits, or to wash clothes. I hardly saw anyone, other than The General and his boy soldiers, but I often snuck a peek out of our tent's door, where I glimpsed a world that resembled a makeshift town. I saw women cooking, girls hauling clothes, and boy soldiers, playing as if they were not The General's prisoners. I longed to get out and stretch in the sunshine, but my place was with the radio, writing out translations, day after day.

One day, a little girl playing outside accidentally kicked an old soccer ball into my tent. The General was out, overseeing the training of the soldiers, so rather than throwing the ball back, I picked it up and beckoned the girl inside. She must have been about ten. Not too old to play with other kids, but not young enough to be safe from The General and his boys. She looked around, as if worried about coming in.

"Please, join me," I said. She stepped in and let her eyes grow accustomed to the dark. She was a little younger than Therese the last time I had seen her. She was skeletal, but her eyes sparkled. She would have been beautiful, were it not for her arm, which looked as if it had been broken and allowed to heal the wrong way. I knew that speaking to anyone other than The General could get me gang-raped, or worse: It could get the girl gang-raped. But I

could not help myself. I had been kept alone, without the opportunity to speak with anyone other than The General for months.
I yearned to touch the little one, to hold her as I would have held
my Therese, but instead, I asked, "What is your name?"

"Sylvia," she whispered shyly. I gave her my name.

"I know who you are," she admitted. I did not know if I had a
reputation around camp, and if so, for what. I did not ask.

"Where is your mama?" She looked at the floor and held her
bent, twisted arm. She shrugged and choked, "Home, I think."

I asked her how long she had been in camp, and it seemed she
was taken from the market the same day I was. She told me that
she wanted her mama, but she did not know if her family was still
alive. I offered her one of the bananas The General had brought
me for my morning meal. She gobbled half of it. We both heard
the arrival of a big truck nearby. With big, wide eyes, she grabbed
her ball and turned to leave.

"Come back tomorrow," I told her as she bolted. I turned to the
tall stack of papers on my desk. I spent my days translating intercepted messages from a stolen radio. By night, I was the receptacle
for soldiers' rage. At every moment I was thinking of my family
and how to get out of the camp. If I could somehow arrange for
someone to deliver a message to Jean-Paul, I could at least let him
know I was alive. I thought about little Sylvia. If I wrote a letter,
could she give it to someone outside of the camp? Would she help
me? I felt guilty for wanting to take advantage of a girl so young
and vulnerable. Maybe I could help her get out too?

My daydreaming ended quickly that day. The General had
returned with the truck and caught me standing with a half-eaten
banana in the middle of the tent. Not working, not listening to the
radio was something he would not tolerate. He grabbed the fruit
from my hand, took a big bite from it, and smashed the rest of it
between his palms. He threw me onto the cot and wrestled me to
my hands and knees. I prepared to think of my husband, about his
twitching toes. It was my usual practice when The General raped

me. That time it was different. He yelled at me, "You don't want to work? I'll make you work!"

He threw open my wrap, and I could hear him behind me, working the fruit onto himself. It made a wet, squishy sound. He forced my legs apart and entered me the wrong way. Instead of thinking of Jean-Paul, I railed at God.

CHAPTER SEVENTEEN

From that day on, I ventured out of the tent more and more. I took chances I should not have, but if it meant getting back to my family, I would do it. I spent more time going to the latrine. I spoke to as many people as I could on the way. While squatting over the hole, I heard from another woman that when The General learned Penda was pregnant, he brought her up the mountain. I could see not one, but two mountains, and it was at least three or four hours walk to each of them from camp. I did not know what The General did on that mountain, but I knew that it was a hard walk, especially for a pregnant woman.

I saw Sylvia, the girl with the broken arm, often. She made a point of stopping by every few days, probably because she was hungry. She said that she would help to deliver a letter from me to my family if I would help her to write one as well. Many of the others in camp could not read or write. Even the boys who had once attended school still had only a basic understanding of French grammar. I wanted to help her, but I had to be careful trusting anybody, much less a child, who might or might not have trustworthy friends.

"I do laundry for the soldiers, and my brother is in camp. He's a scout for The General and goes out often, looking for new recruits," she explained. She thought that if we sent out letters together, her brother might be able to mail them the next time the soldiers went into The City.

"He'd be taking a dangerous chance by carrying mail to The City," I said.

"What could be worse than this?" Sylvia asked me, holding up her arm. I told her I would think about it, but I was nervous about what The General would do if he found out.

—⚹—

One day, while The General was away, I translated a radio communication saying an oil company wanted to hire his militia to take a town near the national park. I did not know how close we were to the park's entrance, but I could see a mountain in the distance, and I knew that would be The General's biggest job. Foreign interests paid him to invade towns, kidnap boys to become soldiers for himself or miners for his brother, The Mole, and turn girls and women into slaves. He would take the foreign payments and set up more camps, while the oil company would move into a vacated village and drill wherever it wanted. The park was a protected place, and it was illegal to drill in or near it, but The General had been taking villages that way for years. It was why he moved us so often. I was in the middle of writing the translation, but I felt an urge to stop. I thought about my own family, about the mess he had made by destroying the market. I thought about Penda, and little Sylvia and Justine, Virgil's mama. No. That was not going to happen again.

What if I never got out? What if he killed me and went on to ruin our country? What if he allowed foreign corporations or others even bigger than himself to take our land and the land of others? I decided that it was the last honest translation I would ever make for him.

I was ashamed at the thought of giving him that transmission. The oil company had been sniffing around our own village for years. They were convinced that the small lake near our farm was full of fuel. Who was I fooling? I knew it was full of fuel. The Volcano had a huge reservoir of underground lava. It also had a supply of methane that, if harnessed, could power Congo for years. The trick, of course, was in knowing how to harvest it. The gas released into the air was toxic and had been responsible for many deaths before. The ash from the last explosion had wiped out people and livestock. It was such a mess. If an oil company wanted to drill near The Volcano and the surrounding lakes, the results could be catastrophic. Jean-Paul and I had talked about it before. The drilling near The Volcano was dangerous enough, but now the oil companies were polluting the lakes. Poisoning our water, killing our fish, uprooting our people, and destroying our ecosystem. How could any local man let that happen to his land? Then I remembered that he was The General. No evil was beyond him. His gleaming white teeth in his perfect smile hid his deep malevolence.

I read and reread the translation I had written and contemplated ripping it up and eating the paper. Then I thought about the possibility of him raping me again, the way he had the last time, and I had to weigh the risks: hand him the paper and risk losing my country or destroy the paper and lose my life. Was there a way out of this? I thought of Sylvia. If I ran, what would happen to her? If I didn't run, what would become of my family?

As it happened, I did not have the chance to give him the translation or to destroy it. He came back to camp with several of the older boys. They were all drunk, celebrating the killing of a silverback gorilla. That kind of poaching meant a lot of money for his soldiers and for him. Although it was illegal, the killing of a gorilla and the distribution of its body parts could fetch a great amount on the black market. I had intercepted a transmission recently that the park rangers had lost track of one of the gorilla families and thought the group had gone to the river to sharpen their teeth on river rocks. And there were the child soldiers, celebrating the death of the adult male. I felt sick at the thought that I had revealed the whereabouts of the gorilla clan just as I had felt sick at telling the soldiers where the best charcoal could be harvested. The harvesting of wood for charcoal, especially near protected land, was only one of many horrible things The General did in order to support his growing army. I turned from my oil company transmission just in time to see a young teenage boy, smeared in blood, fall through my tent's door, clutching a bottle in one hand and a gorilla's severed hand in the other.

"Come on, Mama! General says you're mine this evening!" he said, laughing. He must have been the one who found or killed the silverback. The hand he held had a palm nearly as big as my face. That was not the first time I had had to entertain a teenager. I folded the oil company information and set it under the radio. The boy was so drunk that he could hardly get to his feet. He put the gorilla's hand to his mouth, trying to drink from it, and laughed at himself. I could hear several others outside the tent, shooting their guns into the air and cheering. I thought I might just get lucky enough that the boy would pass out and leave me alone. But to my surprise, he managed to stand. He dropped the gorilla's hand on the desk and pulled me up. He adjusted the radio so tinny music came through the static. He swung me around in a wide arc and pulled me to his pelvis. He groaned and told me, "I miss my girlfriend."

I tried to buy some time and asked him her name. He said she was called Susie. I asked him what she looked like and he grabbed my breast and told me hers were bigger than mine.

"Lucky boy," I said. He laughed and belched. He became serious and said he had planned to ask her to marry him, but when The General came to his town and offered him a job, he took it. He had no education to speak of, and so The General's promise of easy money had been enticing. He said he never knew he would have to kill or rape in order to make a living, but that he had a roof over his head and that was better than nothing. He took a long drink from his bottle and held it out it to me. I took a drink.

"What about Susie?" I asked him.

"If she knew how I felt about her, she might not go off with someone else. But I'm stuck here, doing this," he said, spitting, pointing at the gorilla's fist. I tried to steady him as he pitched forward, nearly pulling me off balance.

"I could help you write to her," I offered. He agreed, and that night I began my new job, not as unpaid prostitute, but as secretary for the soldiers. He cried, telling me his story of being swindled, taken from his family and friends, and forced to work without pay. He closed his letter by explaining to Susie that the moment he got home, they would be married. He thanked me, tucked the letter into his uniform, and fell asleep facedown on my cot. It was not until the early hours of the next morning that I learned his name. But I have forgotten it.

After he left my tent that morning, I folded the oil company information into my wrap. I tiptoed out into the bright sunshine and crossed the camp. I stepped over the passed-out bodies of young drunk soldiers. In the nearest jeep, a woman stared out the windshield at me and removed The General's limp head from her shoulder. As I waited in line with the other women outside the latrine, I could see some children playing near the pigpen. I smiled at Sylvia, who waved at me. Finally it was my turn. When I was inside and alone again, I pulled out the transmission, ripped it into tiny pieces, and threw it into the latrine. The next day, it would be food for the pigs, and nobody would know the difference.

Sometimes The General brought grown men to camp. They were not part of his child army. They were day laborers. He captured local men, who were fathers, sons, and husbands. They were the only grown men I ever saw at camp. He took them as they walked to church, to work, or as they walked their sons to school. He marched them up the nearby mountain in the morning and made them build fences or dig graves, or whatever he pleased. He never fed them and never paid them. At night, they went home. All their work was done at gunpoint. They had no way to avoid that forced labor. Just as we could never leave, they would be bullied like that, many times a week, until we moved our camp.

One rainy day, I was listening to the radio when The General was in our tent, shaving his handsome, evil face. I was never sure if he could speak fluent French, or if he just understood certain words, but he stopped the razor in mid-stroke on his right cheek when he heard the word MONUSCO. It was the French word for the UN. The radio transmission from the park entrance said that MONUSCO helicopters were on their way with the intent of apprehending The General. That was new. I was used to translating information about gorillas, firewood, and other potential resources for The General. It was uncharted territory for me, so instead of writing my translation, I gazed at him and told him what was being said, in real time.

"They said they are heading up the mountain, but I do not know which one he means," I told him. He still clutched the razor, as he leaned over me. The batteries in the radio were always running out, and that day was no exception. He swept the air with the razor, dangerously near my face and yelled, "Translate! Translate! Which mountain is it?"

The radio got quieter and quieter and I could not hear any better than he could. I did not know if the man on the other end spoke of The Mountain or The Volcano, but I knew it was nearby. He flew into a rage, threw the radio onto the ground, ripped off my dress and got on top of me. Before I knew what happened, he slapped me hard and bit off the tip of my nipple. He spat it on the ground next to me. After months of being raped by him, I had gotten used to blocking him out of my mind. He ceased to have power over me. I was outside my body. But when he damaged me like that, I felt it. I tried to scream, but he was louder than I was.

"Clean up this fucking mess!" he bellowed, jumping off me. I was lucky he did not use the razor on me. I scrambled to my feet clutching myself and tried to clean up the radio parts with my free hand. I did not move very quickly, and he kept staring at me in the mirror as I bent to grab the batteries that rolled away. He muttered, "I have to do everything myself," and he plucked the missing part of me off the floor. He marched outside into the drizzle. I followed him to the edge of the tent and saw him throw the piece of my body into the pigs' trough. It became their slop, like so much waste of others. Blood ran down my body onto the floor. I found a piece of cloth near my bedroll and used it to clean the floor and wrap my wound. It was the only bandage I had. The General was outside screaming at someone else about a new radio. The razor in his hand was going to be another person's problem.

As I continued to clean the radio pieces off the floor, I could hear the local men being marched up to camp from the valley below. Instead of being kidnapped to work on a fence, they were ordered to walk through the base and out the back gate. They looked as if they were going in the direction of the nearest mountain. I looked out the door of my tent. There were seven of them: four men and three teenage boys. They all had to empty their pockets of their money, cell phones, and identification on their way past the tent. There was an enormous basket at the corner of the tent where the soldiers collected those things.

One of the men, about Jean-Paul's age, saw me holding my bleeding breast in the doorway. He smiled sadly at me and crossed himself. I swallowed hard. He was a short man with the beginnings of a beard. His sad smile said everything. We were all one tribe under that General. He shook his head as if to apologize.

CHAPTER EIGHTEEN

I wondered why The General needed men from the village to march beyond the camp. Was it the reason he was in such a rage? Why would he bother with the local men when it was so rainy? He must have been doing some new, evil business at the top of the mountain. Were he and his brother starting a new mine? Did they find new trees to cut down? I knew about the gorillas but had not seen any evidence of them other than the silverback they killed. All I knew was that these men would go up the mountain clean and come back down filthy at the end of the day. Suddenly it hit me. It must have something to do with the lost transmission. If MONUSCO were on its way, The General would be on the run. Still why the extra men?

I was puzzling over that, wondering what I would do if the UN came to save me, when I heard a woman shouting. Then another. From my door, I saw an armed teen roughly prodding a naked woman, dressed only in ill-fitting shoes, past my tent. And next, what looked like her daughter, was paraded past. I got very nervous and wanted to tell the boys not to be so rough with the women, but I was bleeding and in pain and scared of what The General would do to me. It seemed like an endless procession of naked women and girls were being marched past me. I saw little Sylvia, with her broken arm, shuffle by. Her shoes were much too large. I stared at the muddy ground. Could I run? The camp was teeming with armed boys.

I worried that would be the end for me. The General might be apprehended, but before he gave up, he would kill us all. He would have to dispose of all the women and children he stole. I began to pray, even though I wasn't sure that I still believed in God. *Please just let me see my family again. Let me get home to my family.*

It was late morning. The rain had turned to a light mist, but at our high elevation, it was colder than in The City. I looked into the treetops at two monkeys who watched me from above. Lucky them, I thought. They can escape into the canopy. The General returned, still half-shaved, still holding his razor. In a rare display of gratitude, he told me, "Thank you for your services, but they are no longer needed."

A young guard came in after him and told me to remove my clothes. I started to take off my bloodstained dress, but The General told me to leave it on. He told the teen, "You see she's had an accident."

"Yes, sir," said the teen, throwing some ill-fitting boots at me. I looked back at The General. He shooed me with the back of his hand. The guard flicked his gun in the direction of the door, and I left.

The sun was trying to peek through the clouds as we crossed fields of young cassava near a village. We passed some farmhouses. Children and women looked nervously out their doorways as we walked by. I assumed that the civilian men who had been marched through the militia base were the husbands and fathers from houses like those. I looked around, realizing that I was grateful to be outside the camp, even though I would probably not live another day. The rolling farmland ended abruptly at the foot of a jungle mountain, which meant we were actually inside the national park. Could The General have been hiding out right under the noses of the government the whole time?

The guard was very young. I wondered where The General found him. I imagined he was about the same age as Therese. Somewhere, if she was still alive, the guard's mama was very worried about him. I turned to face him as I stepped over seedlings.

"Are you from around here?" I asked.

"No," he muttered. He pointed the gun at me. I kept walking. Because it had been raining, the mud between each row of cassava kept sucking my boots off. I stopped to retie them.

"Keep moving!" he barked at me. The mud had filled my boot and squished between my toes. The grit began to slough off the skin from my left foot. My toes hurt.

"Please, may I fix my boot? We'll get there more quickly if I can walk," I said. He seemed to understand and let me tie my boot. It started to rain again, harder. I took the opportunity to look around. A field, a mountain, and a village. We most certainly were in the national park. I had heard stories of The General's men camping out where there would be animals nearby that they could sell on the black market. Gorillas, water buffalo, elephants.

The people in the villages near base were rumored to be of strong stock. Generation after generation had had their land destroyed by The Volcano and every time it happened, they rebuilt. Was the soldier from around there? If I ran from him, would he let me go? Would the villagers agree to shelter me? Probably not; God only knew if they had family members in the militia, or if they were simple farmers, like me.

I addressed the young soldier as "son" and asked him, "How old are you, *mwana*?"

"Shut up! I'm not your son!" he yelled at me, sounding scared. He was the one with the gun. He had no reason to fear me, so I tried again. I said, "You could be my son."

I was not afraid of the boy. If I was going to die because I called him "son," at least I would die in relative comfort, not after hiking up the mountain. He probably missed his family as much as I missed mine. I told him, "You don't have to do this. The General can't raise you as well as your mama can."

"Shut up, Luna," he said.

My God, he knew my name! I had a name once. I was someone. He was also someone with a name. He flicked his gun at me.

I slid through the sucking mud and tried to keep the rain off my face by whisking it away with my hand. The village was behind us. In front of us was the end of the field and the beginning of the forest. I was fairly sure he could not shoot me there, given that we were so close to the village. Once we got to the jungle, he could do what he wanted. He could rape me, shoot me, or let me go.

The rain got stronger, and my dress clung to my bleeding chest. Ahead was an electric fence. The boy soldier said, "Don't touch it. The current will kill you."

"Why does that matter? Am I going to die today anyway?" I asked him. He did not answer. He was busy using his boot and gun to separate the electric wires. I passed through, and as I did, I looked at his face. He had a gap between his teeth and was missing part of one eyebrow. He did not look familiar to me, but I asked him anyway, "What's your name?"

He passed through the fence and ignored my question. Over the months I spent with The General, I had earned a reputation for being a good communicator. Years of being exposed to English and French had made me that way. The only way the gift of mine flourished was through practice, with Therese and with Felix. I knew that my children would need to know languages, so we were always practicing. That is why I survived with The General when others died. I thought maybe the boy knew me through the market or the church on the Long Road, but even at The General's post, I had a reputation. It had become common for boy soldiers and other concubines to come to my tent and ask me to write letters for them. I was lucky that I had never been caught. It could have meant the end of my life, but I thought that if I offered kindness to others, maybe my kindness would be repaid. Had I written a letter for the boy?

We started through the forest. Instantly we were out of the mud. It was difficult to feel the rain, as the foliage around and overhead shielded us. The soldier and I started out by pushing bushes and tree branches out of the way with our hands, but it was nearly impossible to get through the wall of green. He pulled a machete from a pouch on his shoulder and hacked his way though. There was a rough path under our feet, where others had walked earlier, but it seemed as though the trees had instantly grown back after they were cleared.

My feet were walking on a mattress of green. I had no idea how deep the branches under us were. My legs kept getting tangled in the vines, and more than once, I started to fall, only to catch myself with a stinging nettle, which caused burning and itching. We walked like that for about two hours up the mountain. The boy soldier never seemed to get tired. I could hear the blood rushing in my ears. My soaked dress had me shivering, while he stayed warm and dry in rain boots and a poncho.

We heard a helicopter overhead, and he forced me down onto the ground as it passed. I could not see through the canopy, but I prayed that it was the UN. The General had lots of money, but no helicopters. For a moment I considered jumping up and screaming, but the trees were so thick, they would never see me. While crouched on the forest's green blanket, I whispered to the boy, "Did I write a letter for you?"

He looked at me, and his mouth dropped open. The gap in his teeth made him look younger than he probably was.

"The General will kill me if I talk to you," he said, looking around nervously.

"How do I know you?" I asked him.

He admitted, "You don't. Felix does. Don't ask me anything else."

My head started to swim. My son, Felix? How did they know each other? Were they in school together on the Long Road? I didn't think so. Church? No. What happened when I was taken from the market? Was it possible that some harm had come to my family at home that day? I wanted to ask the soldier more questions. Where was my family? Was everyone alive? Where was he taking me? I did not like the suspicious look in his eyes.

"*Maji! Maji!*" he yelled suddenly. He jumped up and grabbed me, pulling me off the ground and up a tree. What sounded like a giant rumbling came our way. In the near distance, I saw treetops falling over, uphill from us. A huge wall of water, *maji*, lunged down the mountain in our direction. I heard the bellowing of unseen animals, and hundreds of birds took flight as the new river came plunging down, just a few feet from where we had been crouched. We both panted as we watched the flash flood speed past. If the soldier meant to kill me later, he certainly did not have to save me then.

He helped me scramble down from the tree, and we both stared at the new river carrying small trees, vines, rocks, and sticks down the mountain. Before I could ask him why he had saved me, he reached into his pocket and handed me a piece of paper. It was old, stained and faded. He said, "Take it before it gets wet."

Written in my son's sloppy script was, *I am here. Felix.*

"*Asante sana*," I said, thanking him. A change seemed to come over him as we continued uphill together. We tried to climb up the mountain near where the river cut through, but the ground kept shifting under our feet. As he whacked his machete through the prickly bushes, he told me about how Felix had been taken by The General and forcibly conscripted into his militia. Felix had no proficiency for violence and guns, but he was used as a translator for The Mole. The boy soldier, whose name I learned was Manny, had been in The Mole's mine for months with Felix. Just weeks before, The Mole had been taken by the UN, and some organization called Free Child Slaves had freed most of the child miners and taken them to nearby shelters. As far as Manny knew, the last news of Felix was that he was alive and in the hospital in The City. He had not heard anything about Therese or Jean-Paul.

Between vines and trees and mud and river, I made an effort to get as much information from Manny as I could. I told him I loved him for helping me and for telling me about Felix. There was so much more I wanted to know.

I asked, "If the miner boys were freed, what are you doing here?"

"My mama is still here," he said. "I killed a militia boy for this uniform. The General told me to put you into the starving pit on the mountain, but I can't do it. My mama is a concubine for The General, and I'm looking for her at the top of the mountain. You'll help me, right?"

My mind started working hard. If the boy was just impersonating a soldier and did not mean to hurt me, why could I not leave? He probably did not have any idea how to use his stolen gun. But if I left, would I die on the mountain anyway? I had been taken far enough away from home that I could not find my way back if I tried. The mountains were crawling with militia groups and poachers. Even though I knew Felix was in The City, it would take me days to get there. Then I thought about Manny and how he had stolen, killed, and lied, in order to find his mama, and I was reminded that my own family was probably doing the same, looking for me.

"I'll help you, but we will have to work together, as a team," I told Manny. "If we find your mama, she'll be part of our team, if she's able. I don't know how we're going to get off this mountain, but we will have to do it together."

He nodded and said, "They told me you'd help me."

He explained that he knew Sylvia, the girl with the broken arm. Her brother, a scout for The General, had been a schoolmate of Manny's. I asked him about the letters I had asked her to pass on to her brother, but he did not have any information about them. All he knew was that there was a woman living with The General who could read and write and help people communicate with their loved ones on the outside. He must have thought, that because I received all The General's communications, I knew exactly where his mother was. He was wrong. But I could not tell him that, because on that rainy jungle mountain, so far from home, Manny was all I had.

—⟶⟵—

We continued slowly. The air was heavy with the afternoon's moisture, and the prickly nettles stung our faces, but still, we climbed. I did not know what we would find at the top of the mountain, but I knew I was not going back where I came from.

"We'll ambush them and take my mother back," Manny explained, but it made no sense. How were we, a boy and an injured concubine, going to sneak up on armed militia? I told him I did not think we would be successful. He reminded me about the drinking habits of the militia boys, especially late in the day.

"From what I saw, they came back from the mountain completely drunk all the time. If they're drinking now, we may have a chance. My uncle, Herve, gets taken almost every day up the mountain. He says they make him work all day, and by suppertime, the soldiers are falling down the mountain. Do you know him? He's short, with a beard?"

I thought about the men who marched up the mountain past my tent. I remembered the man with the beard, who crossed himself and smiled at me. Yes, I knew who he was.

"He has a kind face," I told Manny. I began to think that the boy's plan might work. If the women, children, Uncle Herve, and alcohol conspired against the soldiers, we could have a chance.

The hike was very difficult, and sometimes we needed to crawl on our hands and knees. At one point, the boulders were so large that Manny had to scramble ahead and help me to climb up. I planted my left foot on the rock and grabbed his hand with both of mine. With his machete slung over one shoulder and the machine gun over the other, he was rather unsteady, and as I brought my right leg up, my left slid out from under me and buckled sideways. An audible *pop* came from the left knee, and I cried out as my right knee slammed into the rock. Manny dragged me up, and I sat on the rock with him, clutching both knees.

I surveyed the damage. The right knee was badly bruised and swelling, but something was very wrong in the left one. Something inside did not feel right. I tried to straighten it. Manny shook his head in defeat. Red ants filed toward us, looking for food. We both stood up quickly, afraid to be bitten. I barely made it to my feet when the left knee buckled under me again. He grabbed me and kept me standing.

"We have to move. We need to be back down the mountain by dark," he told me.

"Okay. I'll try." I clutched his shoulder for support. I looked up through the trees and guessed it was midday. If I were not injured, we probably could have made the top by midafternoon and been back down by supper. But with the bad knee, the unstable footing, and the militia soldiers at the top, it was in God's hands.

We reached a dry streambed that had not been affected by the earlier flood. The hill flattened out and we enjoyed a small rest. Manny sat on a rock, and I joined him. He noticed that my left leg was swelling down from the knee into my boot. I removed the mud-coated thing and was surprised that my smallest toenail had turned purple. Normally I would have known immediately that my toe was bruised, but the pain in my knee distracted me. I removed the other boot, and sure enough, the right smallest toenail was also bruised. He laughed and said, "Next time, I'll find you boots that fit!"

I laughed along with him until we both heard rustling in the bushes. He pulled me onto the ground behind the rock. We waited for the militia group to attack. He unshouldered his gun and aimed for the bushes. Suddenly a small, wrinkled hand appeared through the branches. I peered into the bush and realized that gorillas were watching us. The baby ventured into the clearing first, followed by its mama. The babe was brave. He toddled up to us. Manny held tight to his gun, not trusting the creature. The mama gorilla held the baby's hand, much like any mama would. The baby, curious when he found my boot lying on the ground, picked it up and stuck the shoelace in his mouth. I was so taken by the baby that I was surprised when I heard a deep grumbling from the bushes. The mama grumbled back, as if to soothe her family members. I pushed Manny's gun down and smiled at him. He looked up into the nearby tree and saw the gorillas gazing down at us. He looked at me and shrugged.

The baby gorilla found my other boot and investigated it. I wondered how I was going to get my boots back, but I did not have to wonder long, as he had a short attention span and dropped them quickly. Moments later, several other juveniles and older gorillas joined the mama and baby. The deep grumbling came from the woods again, and then the silverback arrived. He was the most enormous animal I had ever seen. His head was as big around as a bicycle tire, and he probably weighed as much as ten men. He moved slowly and quietly and never took his eyes off of us. I kept my eyes down at the ground. He passed me and followed his family to the dry stream, where they began sharpening their teeth on the river rocks.

I counted eighteen gorillas. How could anyone kill such majestic animals, I wondered. They were so peaceful and so like us, it would be madness to harm them. We stayed for many minutes with the gorillas, but both of us knew that although we would have liked to, we could not stay forever. The truth was that for those few moments, I felt freer than I had in months. I felt the connectedness of all living things, honored to be among those creatures and the rocks and trees and mud that made up my Africa. I yearned to be with my family, but I knew that if gorillas could survive in the jungle, so could I. My determination to go on grew with each moment. I put the boots on and followed Manny back into the woods.

CHAPTER NINETEEN

Every step was awkward. The throbbing in my knee gave way to a feeling that something had come loose in the joint. When I turned my foot as I stepped, I would start to fall. Manny took pity, hacked a small tree down with his machete, and made a walking stick for me.

I planted my stick as I put my bad leg down. It was a poor substitute for a human limb. I had to concentrate to stay upright. The opportunity for us to converse had passed. We were approaching the top of the mountain and were nervous about what we would find. Every few minutes, it seemed, helicopters flew overhead, and I was sure it was the UN tracking The General's men—until I made a real effort to squint through the trees. I was surprised to see that the helicopter was black and not the usual white of MONUSCO. I tapped Manny's shoulder and pointed up. He shrugged at me, as if he were just as confused as I was.

My stomach was empty, and I was sure his was too. It was hard to get to the top of the mountain, with a throbbing knee and a growling stomach. My mind drifted to images of home. Therese boiling the night's cassava, Jean-Paul going over Felix's English with him, and I imagined myself returning to my family. I could all but smell the cook fire. Then I realized I could smell smoke. I was not imagining it. The closer we got to the top, the more acrid the smell became. It reminded me of a smell I knew, of burning wood and melted stone. With one hand, I grasped my walking stick, and with the other, I pulled the end of my dress over my mouth.

We both heard screams in the distance, off to our right and uphill. Manny whispered, "Mama!" and took off running. I tried to keep up with him, but it was impossible. I limped along as fast as I could, but I could barely walk. The screaming got louder and more high-pitched, and I realized that Manny was running in the direction of shouting people. Surprisingly I did not hear gunfire. I eventually made my way to where he stood. In a clearing at the top of the mountain, I saw a grate in the ground. Surrounding the bars over the grate were hundreds of pairs of shoes, evidence of those who, over the course of months, had been put into the pit to starve. Standing over the grate were some of the men I had seen marched up the mountain earlier in the morning, including the short man with the sad smile who had made the sign of the cross, Manny's uncle, Herve.

In the distance, I saw the source of the smoke—The Volcano. It was miles away, but still dangerous. If it blew, the entire area could be buried under its lava. Manny made a hasty introduction about me to Herve as I looked around and into the grate. It seemed as though the soldiers had fled and left the village men and prisoners at the top of the mountain. The men could leave, but there was no way out for the women and children in the underground cell, crying under our feet. They were in the path of The Volcano.

Herve cried, "The key to the cell is with the soldiers!" He grabbed the gun from Manny and leveled it at the grate. He told the women inside to back up, and he shot the lock off the hatch. There was a collective gasp from inside the cage. I assisted Herve and the others as well as I could to get the women and children out of the cell. Manny and Herve grabbed one of the women tightly, and she wept in their arms. That must be Manny's mama, I thought. Next to emerge was Sylvia. Her ribs poked out from beneath her skin, and without any clothes to hide it, the break in her arm looked more severe. Most of the women had no clothes, other than the boots they had walked in. Uncle Herve gave his shirt to his sister, and the rest of the men and boys donated their shirts, but some of the women were left without anything to wear. Manny's mama pointed at Sylvia and nudged him in her direction. He removed his poncho and gave it to the little girl. She smiled shyly, as he removed his stolen shirt and donated it to another woman.

There was a long, low rumble, and the ground trembled under our feet. We looked across the valley at The Volcano. It was barely visible beneath the smoke. We would have to leave or get covered in volcanic ash or worse, lava. The helicopter passed overhead again, and we could see a white man leaning out of the door. He held a camera and pointed it at us. Manny waved his hands frantically and yelled, "Help us!"

Soon all of us were yelling for help and waving. Including the village men and boys, we numbered about twenty. I looked down into the empty hole once more and counted the girls and women. The cell looked like it could only hold four people comfortably, yet more than a dozen had emerged. My mind started to race. If The Volcano had erupted while they were locked underground, they could have all perished. That was probably The General's intent, to starve them and destroy the evidence without wasting any bullets.

The helicopter turned a small circle and descended to the clearing. Those of us who had clothing shielded our eyes from the wind that the helicopter stirred up. The white man emerged from the helicopter and ran to where we huddled. He yelled to be heard over the blades.

"Does anybody speak English?" he shouted. I raised my hand. Everyone besides Sylvia and Manny stared at me. I looked at my feet in their enormous boots.

"The Volcano's unstable!" he yelled. I translated into Swahili for everyone. He explained that he had room for twelve adults or fifteen children in his helicopter, and that he could drop them at the airport in The City, but that he was not sure if he could return for the rest. How was I to translate that? If I told those people that only fifteen could go, there would be a fight over the spaces in the helicopter. I thought about the fact that most of the women and girls had been abducted and taken far away from their families, as I had. And most of the boys and men were from the village in the park. To put them on a helicopter to The City would be removing them from their home. The only fair thing to do was to allow women and children on the helicopter, while the boys and men walked down. But that meant walking through militia territory at night, with The Volcano at their backs.

"Come on! Let's go!" the white man yelled. I translated to the group. Immediately the men and boys helped all the women onto the helicopter. It was understood that they had been through so much, raped, stripped of their dignity, and put in terrible conditions. The women inside beckoned to the men and boys to follow them, and most of them jumped in. Soon the only people remaining were Manny, his mama, Uncle Herve, Sylvia, and me.

"Don't you want to come? Some of the locals can get out!" the white man said to me.

"I made it up this mountain. I can make it down!" I yelled. He climbed into the flying machine and called, "Good luck!"

He handed us several water bottles and some candy bars. I turned to little Sylvia, who looked as if her poncho swallowed her. She took my hand. I pointed to the helicopter, and she shook her head.

"I'm coming with you," she said, patting my hand. I wondered if I had made a mistake in not getting on the helicopter, but I knew that our chances of making it back to safety were much improved by having food, water, and each other's company. I also knew that families needed each other and splitting this one up so that any one of them was alone would be a bad thing. Sylvia had grown up with Manny and his mama as neighbors. For all I knew, her relatives could be dead, so these neighbors might become her family.

We watched the helicopter depart into the smoky sky. My heart sank as I thought about my own family, who would have to wait to see me again. I felt foolish, as I thought about my knee and how much it would hinder us on the way down. Did I put those people in more danger by not getting in the helicopter? How would we find our way, and what would await us at the bottom?

"We need to go back another way. It is too dangerous down by the camp," Herve said, handing out better-fitting shoes and boots to the women. "We've been living in this park for years, and we know all of the downhill trails."

I wondered if he was telling the truth, especially when he pointed the way we were going. It seemed we were headed straight to The Volcano. My knee protested, and I limped more severely after standing still. Herve offered his elbow, and I shooed him off, too proud to accept help. We drank our water and ate our candy bars in silence. The only sounds were the rumbling volcano and the slashing of Manny's machete.

"I am Roho," said Manny's mama after we had been walking for a while. She was so thin. Herve's shirt hung on her as if it were covering a skeleton. Her eyes bulged from her face, but she smiled in spite of hunger and exhaustion. She clung to Manny's elbow for support.

"You have a good boy," I said, complimenting her.

We all had slavery stories to share. The General had turned Uncle Herve into a workhorse, had made Manny a murderer, and used Roho, Sylvia, and me for his manly pleasures. Under The General, we had something in common. Terror fuses people together. I was sure that Felix was recuperating safely in a hospital in The City, but I had no idea what fate had befallen Therese or Jean-Paul. I prayed silently that if they were separated from each other they each had found a caring temporary community, as I had.

We trudged through the dense forest. Luckily there was a clear animal trail that wound through the trees. I had to avoid stepping in very large droppings. They did not resemble what the gorillas left behind, so I asked Uncle Herve about the animal that deposited them.

"Buffalo," he guessed. "It's more than one, so we don't really have to worry. We would be in trouble walking around here if there were just one."

I was aware that buffalo could stampede, and I did not understand until he explained that a solitary buffalo feels vulnerable and can charge unrelentingly at an interloper. Many people in the area feared losing their lives on the horns of a buffalo. I shivered as I thought about the oncoming darkness, The Volcano, the militia, the wild animals, and my limp. As if reading my mind, Herve said, "Manny and I can carry you."

The group stopped and awaited my answer. Little Sylvia clutched my hand and prompted me. I looked around at the expectant faces, urging me to accept. I knew that in the past, many dead people had to be carried out of The General's underground jail. I thought about Sylvia and Roho and the other women starving in the cell and being carried to a nearby grave. There was no way anyone was going to carry me if I was still alive. The only way I would be carried out of the forest was if I were dead.

"No, thank you. I'll walk. If I slow you down, you can leave me," I told him.

"You're one stubborn woman," whispered Roho, patting me on the shoulder.

"You can carry me!" Sylvia chirped. Manny crouched down and let Sylvia jump on his back. She weighed next to nothing, but he still groaned with the effort. Only when I saw that Sylvia was tended to, did I allow Herve to give me his arm. Between my walking stick and his elbow, I almost felt as if I could walk normally. Roho hummed a familiar tune, and Herve and Manny joined in. It took my mind off our situation to puzzle out where I had heard that song. Maybe it was something the children in the choir sang at the church on the Long Road. We went on like that for quite a while until a terrible sound made us freeze in mid-step.

It was an explosion, someplace off to our left, and it appeared as if the entire jungle had heard it. Chattering birds quieted. It was so still that the trees seemed empty of their inhabitants. Then something in the forest keened like a baby. It sounded as if it was being tortured or eaten. Thousands of creatures descended the mountain. We quickened our pace, heading to the right, but had no idea what was coming from behind. Manny tried to keep up with his mother but had the burden of Sylvia on his back. Herve pulled me along forcefully into the dense forest. If I had been lost and disoriented already, I was hopeless then. I tried to plant my walking stick and keep up with him, but I dropped it, and with both hands, I clung to his elbow.

Suddenly a giant ball of hot rock landed on our left. It hit a tree and burst into flames. The forest around it began to burn, and we ran. Sylvia screamed as Manny rushed her through burning branches, while I clenched against the pain as Herve gathered me to his side, my feet barely touching the ground. After an agonizing hour of running, we appeared to be much lower down, but could still smell burning trees. Herve guided us toward some large boulders, and we sat on the downward slope to rest for a moment. None of us spoke. We could hear gunfire on the other side of the mountain. There was a battle being waged against The General's militia outpost. I smiled as I thought about the MONUSCO transmission I failed to translate. The others stared at me as if I were crazy. With hellfire raining all around us, and the darkness falling, I was smiling.

It was contagious. Herve started to laugh, and then his sister joined in. Then Manny and Sylvia. We sat like that, eating melted candy bars and watching the fiery boulders crash and burn around us. We could hear screams from the distant outpost, but none of us knew if they were under siege from The Volcano or the UN. I ceased worrying about everything. I think the others felt it too. There were so many ways to die in Congo. And there we were, alive.

Through the trees in the distance, where the forest ended, I could see blackness and more blackness, as far as my vision could reach. My mind told me it was crops leading to the highway, but my eyes told me otherwise.

"It's the lake," explained Herve. I was confused because the only big lake I knew was The City's Lake and it was two hours' drive from my home. Could it be that we had ended up right where we started? If this was The City's Lake, where were we?

"Get us out of here," Roho suggested. Herve helped me up, and Manny hoisted Sylvia on his back. Slowly, *pole pole*, we made our way through the remaining forest. The ground flattened out, and there was a visible path through the dried mud. The smoke from The Volcano obscured any stars or moon that we might have used to light our way. I relied on Herve and was grateful I had him with me. He and Manny had saved many lives that day by freeing the girls and women from the cell. It was probably under burning lava by now. If it had not been for Herve, I might have been stuck on the mountain when The Volcano erupted. If Manny had not pulled me from the outpost, I might still be there in the crossfire between the UN and The General, or between The General and The Volcano. I thought about my battered knee and decided it was a small price to pay for my survival.

As we neared the lake, I was surprised to see a large boat docked near a small pier. There did not seem to be any electricity on the pier, but the ship glowed. Before I asked, Manny questioned Herve, "What is that?"

Herve laughed, "I do not know, but it's better than the mountain!"

CHAPTER TWENTY

T he Floating Hospital was unlike anything I had ever seen or heard of. A massive ship, it had once been used to take wealthy white people on tours of the African Great Lakes. A *mzungu* named Dr. Mecklenberger bought it and raised money to convert it into a hospital. She was aware that people in the remotest areas of Africa often did not have access to good medicine, so rather than have patients limping into The City on foot or traveling through the dangerous jungle, she brought the medicine to them.

Dr. M had long, black-turning-white hair that even in a braid fell all the way down her back and nearly to her waist. Tattoos trailed down her arms from under her scrubs. Her eyes were filled with sadness, although her words came out positive and happy. The first time I met her was when she greeted me as I entered the hospital from the gangplank. She stood in the doorway with a very short security guard and a female orderly.

"*Jambo*, Mama," the doctor said. I told her I spoke English, and she laughed.

"You make my job easy," she said. She looked at me leaning heavily on Herve. Behind us, Roho and Sylvia were barely propped up by Manny. He was so weak and tired that he shuddered under their weight. It was late at night, and the doctor seemed unused to receiving patients at that hour, especially those who came in groups. The inside of the ship whirred with a machinelike rhythm, but other than the medic and her two helpers, there were no other signs of life. The doctor's pitying eyes took us in. Roho and Sylvia, both dehydrated, probably appeared the worst, although the rest of us stank of smoke, sweat, blood, and fear. The doctor glanced down at my knee and up at my chest. I had forgotten about the stains on my dress.

"Were you shot?" she asked me. I told her I had been bitten.

"By a snake?" she asked.

"By a man."

She asked if the man had hurt the other two, and I told her, yes, he had. She glanced at Sylvia in the poncho and Roho wearing her brother's shirt and turned her sad eyes on the short security guard.

"Mbegu, raise the gangplank and wake the others," she ordered. Within moments, the boat roared to life. Somewhere below, there was a beehive of sleeping crew members who, at the signal of the queen bee, flew into action. As blankets and water were brought to us, the female orderly wrote down our names, where we were from, and a description of our medical conditions.

"My name is Fuhara. Welcome." She smiled warmly. Her name meant beauty in Swahili. Her teeth gleamed white in the fluorescent lights. I thought about Therese, out there on dry land. I looked at this young beauty and wanted so much for Therese to learn and to grow in a peaceful Congo where she could go to school and grow up to have a good job like Fuhara. It was hard to concentrate on my own health when there was fighting and fire outside on the mountain. My mind raced. I wondered about The General and where he was.

"There are four doctors and a nurse on the ship tonight. They'll take care of you, but first, we need to move farther out into the lake . . ." she started to say. I interrupted her and told her, "My family is out there."

The orderly crouched down next to me. She explained that the reason they had been docked where they were was because it was unclear if the lava flow was going to damage The City. They were nearby to support the hospitals there. As of yet, they had not seen any other patients, but due to the violent nature of some of our injuries, they needed to move away from the shore. In other words, they did not want to be boarded by The General's men.

"My son is in the hospital in The City," I started to say. I was going to add that I needed to get to him, but I knew Fuhara was right. I would not last two hours in the dark alone. With my knee the way it was, I could hardly walk across the examining room. Frustrated, I started to cry. The white-and-black-haired doctor took Fuhara's place, crouched down, and took my hand.

"I know it's hard being separated from your kids," she said. "We have a great communications team onboard. I can check with The City hospitals and ask about your family. Give me their names, and I'll find out what I can." I nodded and glanced at the others. A tall, balding white man with glasses and a white coat was speaking with Roho and Sylvia. Fuhara translated as Herve and Manny looked on with concern. The balding man held Sylvia's broken arm and pointed down the hallway.

"She'll be well cared for here. Don't worry," Dr. M told me. I explained that little Sylvia did not know the fate of her family. I was not worried about her in the Floating Hospital; I worried about what might come next for her after she left.

"That always worries me the most too," Dr. M admitted.

That night was one of the strangest of my life. Our little community of The General's refugees was tended to by many caring foreigners. The tall, balding man, Dr. Donnelly, treated me for injuries The General had inflicted. He cleaned and sewed up the wound on my breast and administered a strong medicine that would keep at bay the HIV illness The General had caused in me. Dr. Donnelly had two daughters back in America and one was the same age as my Therese. He had a special way of frowning and smiling at the same time. I started to get used to the way white doctors looked at me; he had the same sad smile as the black-and-white-haired doctor. She was the one who ordered the images of my knee. I tried to lie very still as the massive machine took pictures of my body. I was nervous about it falling on me and crushing my leg, and I shook with chills and fear. I felt trapped and had a hard time breathing, as if caught in a cave. Although Dr. M had ordered that we all be given medical care, water, and food, the doctor had perhaps overlooked the anxiety we all felt after being put through the rigors of rape, kidnapping, and slavery. She was all about fixing our bodies and getting us back to our lives.

The doctor did have a support staff of trained listeners. She had brought Nurse Carp to speak to us. The nurse cried every time she heard our stories. After my stitches and imaging, Nurse Carp found her way to my room. She had been crying, after hearing Sylvia's tale of how The General had broken her arm while he thrust his privates into her mouth. She was dabbing her eyes when she came to my bedside. I lay in a comfortable bed with my tightly wrapped knee elevated on two soft pillows. She pulled up a chair and took my hand. Her greasy, light-brown hair fell into her eyes.

"Do you want to talk?" she whispered.

I told her all about the day I was taken from the market, and about my life away from my family with The General.

"What do you know about your loved ones?" she asked.

"Felix, my son, is in a hospital in The City," I started to say. She shook her head and said, "I'm afraid I have bad news about your husband."

Then she told me that from the information they had collected from The City, my husband was dead. But not only dead, completely taken apart by The General's army. His remains had been found in a gravesite behind what used to be our village. Everyone could hear the keening sounds of fury, grief, and sickness that came from my room when I heard the news. Jean-Paul was such a good man. He was smart and kind and provided for his family and the children of the village. When I thought that the rapist who used me for months had ordered the massacre of innocent

Jean-Paul, it shattered my heart. Nurse Carp cried with me. She held me in her arms, and I wept on her shoulder.

When the tears were over, she told me the good news.

"Not only is Felix alive, but Therese is too."

Our dear friend, Mr. Muhangi, had been in contact with Therese and had looked after Felix and Virgil. It was so emotional, hearing about Jean-Paul and then about my children. I wanted to get up and jump off the ship, but the nurse assured me that I was far too injured to go anywhere, especially in the middle of a crocodile-infested lake.

The black-and-white-haired Dr. M came in. Seeing me hugging Nurse Carp, she said, "I have more good news for you. The connective tissues in your knee were not torn, but they were severely sprained."

I would be in a hinged brace for eight weeks while I got my strength back. I would also need to stay on the medicine for the disease The General gave me, probably for the rest of my life. My chest would heal, but I would always have an ugly scar.

Herve came to my bedside every day and helped me put on my shoes so that I could get up and walk a bit. It was hard to put on socks when I wore my brace, so he helped me with those too. "I just did this for Sylvia also," he said jokingly, pulling up my sock. *This is a good man*, I thought. He had never married, and had no children of his own, and I began to think that if Sylvia never found her family, maybe he could take care of her. I suggested this, but apparently Herve had already made those arrangements. He was experienced in that part of Congolese life. When Dr. Donnelly came in one day to check on me, he was followed by Fuhara, the orderly, who had a stack of papers for Herve to sign.

"This is why I get paid the big bucks," Dr. Donnelly said laughing. "Doctor by night, lawyer by day." I wondered how much the doctors got paid to be there, caring for brutalized people in Congo.

Because I had already trusted him with my life, I did not feel awkward asking.

"I actually don't get paid for being here," he answered. "I'm
doing it as a favor for Dr. Mecklenberger. I guess you could call me
a volunteer." He and the others had left their families, sometimes
for months at a time, to go there to a war zone and help. I could
feel the tears well up in my eyes. He hugged me as I thanked him.

—⋙—

We had been in the hospital for close to a week. It was clear
to us that we could not go back to The City. With Roho in failing
health and the rest of us healing well, Herve, Manny, Sylvia, and
I began to feel restless. Dr. Donnelly and Dr. M called a meeting
with us over dinner one night. We were anchored in the middle of
the lake. The generator hummed, and the lights flickered against
the mahogany walls of the dining room. I chewed on a chicken leg
and wondered why all the fuss about calling a meeting.

Dr. Donnelly explained, "We're getting low on supplies, and
we can't go back to The City because it's too unstable. There's a
women's shelter across the lake where Luna can go, but Roho really
needs a more stable hospital to help her with her . . . condition."

The black-and-white-haired doctor put it bluntly. "We don't
know where to put the rest of you," she said.

That seemed to be one of the problems with my country. If you
were hurt, you could get fixed in a hospital, but then what? Sylvia's
brother, the scout, was still on the run with The General. With a
battle going on, no home, and no family to receive them, Herve,
Manny, and Sylvia would be on their own. The very loose plan was
for them to be given enough money to get to the IDP camp on a
bus. There was something wrong with that. It made me uneasy to
think of them on a bus in the middle of militia territory. I tried to
picture Sylvia with her arm in a sling, on a dangerous road with
Manny and Uncle Herve.

"I do not know what to say. I am glad to have the opportunity to be in a women's shelter, but what about the others? What about my family?" I asked. Right then Fuhara barged into the dining room below decks. She carried a laptop and ran in my direction. She blurted out that she was sorry to interrupt, but that she just received some video footage from the communications team. Five or six Congolese crew members from the communications department ran in behind her. They looked so different from everyone else, who wore white coats or scrubs. They were a plainclothes team I had not known existed before then. Even Mbegu, the night guard, joined us in the dining room. Fuhara knelt down next to me. She shoved aside my plate and put the laptop in front of me.

"This comes from Dr. Bingi in The City. He works with a film and video organization called Free Child Slaves. I think you'll want to see this," she said, panting. On the screen was a handsome, one-legged boy standing and giving testimony about his dead brother, and suddenly I saw something amazing. There was my Therese, saying she was looking for her family and not to forget about her. She spoke perfect English, the English we had been practicing for years. And she was strong and beautiful. But more important, she was alive! The crew around me patted me on the back, and Dr. Donnelly squeezed my shoulder. Predictably Nurse Carp cried.

"Where is she?" I asked. The footage was weeks old. The last they heard, she had been staying at a women's shelter near our church, but she had since moved from there, and no one was quite sure where she was now. I had so many questions. How could I get to her? Was it safe for me to go to where she was? Where would we live if there was no village left?

The rest of my time on the boat was a blur. All I could think about was Therese and how I might be able to see her soon. It was like torture, being on a boat all the way across the lake from her, but I knew that if she were brave enough to speak on camera, she was brave enough to find me. I am not sure how many days we were on the boat before I made it to the dock on the other side, but two very important things happened during those days.

First, Roho died. Because she was treated too late, the HIV that The General gave her killed her. There were sores all over her body, and she had lost so much weight. It was unbelievable to me that she could suffer such torture at his hands, hike out from the underground cage on the mountain, and endure being away from her family, only to ultimately die from an infection. I mourned her loss with Manny and Herve, who had tried so hard to keep her alive. Herve paced up and down the length of the boat, crying. I wanted so much to comfort my kind, new friend, but all I could do was make him stop pacing and put his head on my shoulder.

I prayed with the doctors and the crew during the makeshift memorial ceremony. Manny cried for his mother and held my hand. I could not cry anymore. The General could not hurt me on that ship, or so I thought.

The day after we put Roho's body into the ship's morgue, I awoke feeling queasy. It had been a rough night on the ship, and many of the doctors and crew were seasick. There were seasick bags stuck into all the handrails on the stairways and hallways, and nobody seemed immune to using them. But after everyone had recovered their normal skin tone, I stayed sick. Especially in the morning. I thought about my last menstrual period, and that convinced me. Nurse Carp found me throwing up over the edge of the boat that day.

"How long were you with The General and his men?" she asked.

"Long enough to know it is not my husband's," I told her. She rubbed my back, and I said, "I do not care if God does not approve. I am not having this baby."

"I understand, and so does everyone on this boat. It's your body, not The General's and not God's," she said. She clapped her hands once and opened them toward Heaven.

She hugged me as I cried on her shoulder again. The next day, Dr. Donnelly had me sign the papers giving him permission to help me with my problem. And within six hours, The General's hold on me was released forever.

—⁂—

Saying goodbye to Manny, Herve, and Sylvia was one of the hardest things I had done. We had been through so much together. We arrived at the boat as a team and would be leaving separately. I was sure I was going to be well cared for at the women's shelter, but I was nervous about the life that awaited my friends. I asked Herve how I might contact him in the future. He gave me the name of the mechanic shop where he had worked before The General had come to The City, but only God knew if it was still standing. I told Herve about the church on the Long Road, but who knew its fate?

As the ship pulled into the dock, I was stunned by how many people awaited us. The pier was bustling with people. There were men carrying fish in baskets, children and women with jerry cans of water on their heads, and many people at a makeshift market, haggling for food and other goods. Among those people was a film crew pushing its way through the crowd. A tall man with a camera and a red-haired woman with bright blue eyes barged their way to me. With them was a tall, familiar-looking woman in a too-small dress with flowers on it.

My God, it is my daughter! I thought as I limped down the gangway and into my Therese's arms.

CHAPTER TWENTY-ONE

Therese stopped the camera, put it on the ground, and embraced her mama. Luna rocked Therese back and forth and whispered into her hair, "We've come such a long way."

The women looked out over the cassava field. Luna thought about what happened to them all after she walked off the gangplank. For the two years after New Beginnings, Therese found a comfortable routine as a student at a private high school in a village near the church on the Long Road. She continued to help with the crops at home and occasionally traveled by bus to see Robert, who lived in The City. Then just as *Unnatural Resources* began to get the attention it deserved, Brianna generously offered to send Therese to high school in America for her junior year. It was a mixed blessing for Therese. She finally had the opportunity to see how teenage girls lived in California. She accomplished a lot with Brianna. She was a star on the track team, sang solos in honors choir, and got good grades. But when she returned to Luna from Brianna's home in America, she was no longer satisfied with her life in the Democratic Republic of the Congo. She was not content to haul water and plant crops in her free time. She had been allowed to learn in a proper school and have a social life befitting a teenager. After living in a peaceful, prosperous home in California, the idea of living in a church, with Robert two hours away in The City, did not sit well with her.

One night, after the boys had gone to sleep, she and Luna cleaned the chalkboards in the school with Mr. Muhangi. She complained, "Mama, I hate my life here."

"Perhaps you would like to be in the grave they dug for our village," snapped Mr. Muhangi. Luna put her hand on his shoulder and tried to soothe him, but he was old and contrary, and he pushed Luna's hand away.

"The *mzungu* have spoiled you, Therese," he said mournfully.

Therese countered, "I miss Robert. I want to move to The City to be with him."

Luna said, "It was bad enough being away from you when The General took me, and your time away in America was hard for us."

"You have no idea how I feel!" she shouted, and instantly covered her own mouth. Luna did know how she felt. So did Mr. Muhangi. They had both lost their spouses years earlier.

Soon after, Robert moved from The City to stay with them and help with the cassava harvest. With the help of a sponsor, he'd finished high school and been fitted with a prosthetic leg. With his new leg, he was much more able-bodied. Mr. Muhangi frowned on an unmarried couple living in the house of God, but what were the options? Luna worried about Therese having babies too soon. They had an unspoken agreement that while they were under Luna's roof and eating Luna's food, there would be no babies. Luna had told Therese that as long as she was in school, she did not have to be married. But Congolese men felt it was their right to have a wife and children. It was a point of contention between Robert and Luna. Girls married and had babies young in Congo, but Luna knew her daughter's future potential would be hampered if she bore children too soon.

The sleeping arrangements were awkward. Mr. Muhangi slept with the boys in a classroom on a pile of blankets. Luna had her own nest in the hallway outside. Therese and Robert slept in the pews in the sanctuary. The acoustics were so good that Luna could hear them kissing. Sometimes she overheard their conversations.

"I love you," Therese would whisper.

"I love you more," Robert whispered back. Therese giggled, "Your breath smells like cigarettes. No smoking in the house of God."

"How about sex? Can we have sex in the house of God?" he said with a groan.

"No sex until we have a house of our own."

Good girl, Luna thought. She heard the sanctuary door open and close again. Robert lit up outside, and Luna smelled the smoke that drifted through the windows.

Mr. Muhangi yelled, "No smoking in the house of God!"

Life went on at the church on the Long Road. They missed their village, but they managed as well as they could. Felix and Virgil continued to grow up together as unbrothers. Luna never signed any custody papers for Virgil. It was just assumed that he was hers, and she loved him, even if he was a troublemaker. Mr. Muhangi did his best to tolerate Virgil but claimed that the only reason he let him stay in the church was because of his fishing prowess.

One day as they sat at the table set up by the lake, Therese and Luna cleared away the remains of supper, and Mr. Muhangi asked Virgil, "How do you even make it through a day of school? You can't multiply or divide!"

"I can tell you that you'd have half as much food on this table if it weren't for me," Virgil said, grinning. He pointed at the mountain of fish bones left at their plates.

Felix stared across the lake at the bald spot where the village once stood. An egret soared over the water. He sighed. "After such a nice meal, we should go home, to a proper house to sleep."

For years human rights organizations had fought with the utility company that wanted Luna's land. The organizations insisted that the home and village had been the site of a humanitarian tragedy and that they belonged to the Congolese people. The General had been defeated in the national park, but Luna and her family were still too scared of local gangs to rebuild their home. Their land lay empty.

—⋙—

Therese graduated from her private high school with honors. She had stayed in touch with Brianna and took her up on her offer to pay for Therese's college education. She enrolled in the university in The City and commuted on the bus, two hours each way. There she studied political science and learned about government. Luna was so proud of her. Village girls did not often go to school. She kept up with her studies, returned every night to help cook supper, and got up early every morning to go back on the bus.

One day, with Felix and Virgil in school, and Therese at the university, Robert and Luna found Mr. Muhangi sitting on the steps to the church, with his head in his hands.

"It's time to rebuild our village," he said. "But we have a community of only six. We need more people. We need children to educate." He looked meaningfully at Robert.

"Therese is too young. Don't get any ideas," Luna told them both.

"Mr. Muhangi's not a young man, Luna," Robert said. "Will his legacy be to leave behind a dead village?"

The old man was right. Those who had survived the day the village burned had fled, and without a population, any effort to set down new roots was destined to fail. The General was finally gone, but the damage he had done stayed with them. Luna thought about Herve, Manny, and Sylvia. It had been years since she had seen them. She missed her temporary community on the Floating Hospital. She wondered how they were.

The next day, after Therese, Felix, and Virgil left for school, Robert helped Luna find Herve. Using the computer Brianna had donated to the church, he contacted FCS, who confirmed that Herve's old mechanic shop was still standing in The City. Luna sent him an e-mail at the shop, praying he still worked there. Within a month, he came to visit, arriving on the same bus that Therese rode to and from the university. The first words from his mouth were, "I thought I'd never see you again."

The short visit became a long visit. The days became weeks. Luna thought Mr. Muhangi would have a heart attack when he had not one, but two bachelors sleeping with women they were not married to under God's roof. Herve was the same as he had been the last time Luna saw him. He still had the sad eyes and the half-grown beard. As Luna watched him greet her children when they returned from school each day, she noted the warmth with which he kissed them on both cheeks, and realized that the feeling of gratitude she felt toward him for saving her life had become so much more. Jean-Paul was not the only good man Luna had grown to love in Congo.

One afternoon, Herve and Luna walked down the highway to the market together. The blazing sun on their backs seemed to cook the cassava in their baskets. Luna felt the camaraderie that she had felt when Justine and she used to haul fish to sell. For the first time in what seemed like an eternity, Luna did not feel lonely or scared on that road.

Herve told her, "I had thought that I'd become a ranger in the park."

"Why?" she asked.

"That day on the mountain with you made me realize that people aren't the only ones in danger up there."

Luna asked what made him change his mind.

"I had a life before The General," he said. "A safe life. I thought it would be smarter to stay out of the park. A ranger's life is dangerous. I'm glad I made that choice." He looked at Luna in a meaningful way.

The market was less populated than it had been before The General came. Several stalls remained empty, and it would be a slow business day. Luna set down her basket, and Herve helped her spread the cassava on the ground. He kept her company, and they talked all day about their lives after The General, about their loneliness, about their families.

Mr. Muhangi winked at them when they arrived home that evening. He had already asked Herve to stay. He was only waiting for Luna to realize her feelings for him.

They were married on the sixth of July on a sunny afternoon at the church on the Long Road. Because they did not have a priest of their own, they had to bring in the minister from the next town to officiate. Luna was sure that the first husband and the father of her children would have wanted her to remarry and to be content. But sometimes she still missed Jean-Paul. They had been happy before she was kidnapped, and she never stopped loving him. But Luna understood that the human heart was capable of making space for more than one lover.

Before The General forced him to be a slave laborer, Herve had worked in the mechanic shop on all types of trucks and cars, recycling parts of old vehicles, and using them in new ones. He was very handy and loved to build things. Herve and Robert had become fast friends, and Robert's knowledge of electronics translated well into Herve's vocabulary of auto repairs. Soon they were planning to open a machine and electronics shop.

After Therese, Felix, and Virgil went off to school one day, Herve, Mr. Muhangi, Robert, and Luna were cleaning fish near the lake. Herve gazed at the potholed highway and reasoned, "The roads are so poor out here that someone is bound to get a puncture."

Robert nodded. "When our village gets bigger, people will need a garage," he said.

"Who around here can even afford a car?" Luna asked argumentatively. Mr. Muhangi grunted in agreement.

Herve said, "My sister's husband, Chui, has tons of money. He sold his land to real estate developers. He has two cars and a motorcycle!"

Mr. Muhangi snorted. "You're crazy. We don't even have real electricity. How are you planning to do repairs with just a generator for power? We'll never have enough petrol."

"Therese said Brianna paid to put in solar power at New Beginnings," Robert said. "Maybe she would help us put in solar here?"

Luna looked up at the sun peeking out through the clouds and wondered, *If we had solar power, would we ever run out of energy?*

That night, Therese composed a message to Brianna. Their plans were evolving. They would rebuild their village across the lake, and they would move back home. Before they went to sleep, Brianna had e-mailed Therese back with an offer to help.

Herve reached out to his brother-in-law, Roho's widower, Chui, who brought not only Manny, but also his other six children, to visit. The reunion with Manny was almost as tearful as the one with Herve. Manny had grown from a weak, skinny, gap-toothed teenager to a strong, skinny, gap-toothed young man. They spent a few days with Chui and Manny, but their home was too small to house everyone; there were limited places for them in the church. But before Chui left, Herve had convinced him to move to the village they were rebuilding. Luna had plans for electricity, ideas for businesses, ample food supply, and a church. All they needed was money. And Chui had plenty of it.

Therese, Felix, and Luna gave Chui a tour of what used to be their village on his final day with them. He could easily visualize where the pier would go, where the homes would be, and how they could make the machine shop work. Luna gazed out over the cattails to the lake. The sun reflected magically on the water.

"How is Sylvia?" Luna asked him.

Chui said, "Life has been hard for her. You know, that arm never healed properly, so she has very limited abilities. And her brother, the scout, he didn't make it. He died of pneumonia."

Felix, normally the quiet one, interrupted, "The General hurt all of us. He broke my fingers, he took Robert's leg, and he made Mama sick, but we all do okay."

Therese finished for him and said, "Some of us are doing better than okay."

Luna put her arms around her children and asked them, "So there is room for one more?"

Sylvia arrived shortly after Chui and his family returned to them. Before they knew it, they had a community. They had started construction of a new house for Luna's family, right where their old house had been. It was small, and could barely hold Herve and Luna, plus Therese, Robert, Felix, and Virgil. Chui and his family built a house next to theirs, and the machine shop was built within a few months of that. Mr. Muhangi claimed that living in the house of God was more than satisfactory for him, and he refused to move into his own home. It was just as well; by that time he was so old and grouchy that nobody wanted to live next to him.

With fifteen people in their small community, everyone had to pitch in. Chui, whose name meant "leopard" in Swahili, was a great hunter and brought back all the bush meat they needed. Because Sylvia's arm remained painful, she was in charge of light tasks like feeding the chickens and drying the cassava. Virgil was their fisherman, and it took everything in Luna's power to keep him out of Mr. Muhangi's boat on weekdays, when he should have been at school. He and Felix attended high school together in a neighboring town. Some days, while Felix was still in classes, Luna found Virgil walking back home on the highway.

With everyone living in such close proximity, relationships were bound to develop. Felix began to show an interest in Sylvia when her shy eyes met his after school one day, and Luna knew that was destined to be the next great love.

"You stay focused on your studies. Keep your eyes to yourself!" she urged Felix.

"I can hear Therese and Robert making out through my walls, and they're not even married!" he argued.

"How fair would it be if I let Therese marry Robert before she finishes her education?" Luna said. "Brianna supports Therese in her studies, as long as she stays in school. The same goes for you. If you want Brianna to pay for you, you'd better stay focused on school. The last thing you need is a wife and *watoto* to feed."

That night, while Herve and Robert were away in The City buying supplies for their shop, Luna overheard a terrible row between Therese and Felix.

"Marrying young is an affront to the education Mama and Brianna have sacrificed to give you!" Therese shouted.

"It's none of your business what I do with my girlfriend. Especially since we all know what you do with Robert!" Felix yelled.

The entire compound could hear them fighting, and from across the lake they heard Mr. Muhangi shout, "You all just keep it in your pants and let me sleep!"

In the end, the agreement stuck. Until children had an education and were employable members of the community, there would be no marriage and no babies. There were enough children in the village. Chui had six of them, all grade-school aged, and they were receiving an education from Mr. Muhangi. Manny had a natural way with kids, and although he frequently fought with his younger siblings, they all respected him as their new teacher's helper. Life was never going to return to normal, but they were back on their feet.

CHAPTER TWENTY-TWO

F inally the day came when Therese graduated from college. All fourteen other members of the community were there to see her become the first college graduate in their new village. They traveled on the bus to the university in The City and saw her walk down the aisle with her diploma in hand.

While most of the graduates had family members at the commencement, Therese was the only one with *mzungu* guests. There, in the folding chairs on the university's lawn, were Brianna and her family. Luna thought Therese would never stop crying, she was so happy to see them. She finally got to meet the extraordinary woman who had seen something special in her daughter and who had nurtured her as a second mother.

Therese gushed, "Thank you, Mama Brie, for helping me, and for coming so far!"

Brianna said, "Thank *you* for coming so far!" and they threw their arms around each other. Luna turned and saw a soccer game starting on the lawn. Brianna's boys, both of them tall as reeds, had initiated a match with Luna's own. The older boy, Nate, was able to pick up an easy friendship with Felix. The younger boy, Elliot, seemed rather taken with Virgil, even if several years separated them. They all played as if they had known each other forever.

Alain, Brianna's husband, asked Therese, "What's next for you?"

Therese's brows knitted together in thought. "I know that Robert and my family will always be here," Therese said, "but the land we live on is risky. The only way I know how to keep it and my family safe is to learn more about our rights. So I am going to study law."

"Then it would be my pleasure to help you learn more," Brianna told her.

—ɯ—

With Brianna's financial help, Therese went to law school in The City. On the day of her graduation, the party in the village ran well into the night. The feast that Chui and Virgil made was enough to feed an army. The children ran with sparklers and noisemakers through their town as music blared from a speaker in Herve and Robert's repair shop. Later that evening, Robert approached Luna and asked for her blessing. She gave it to him, and before Luna knew it, he was on one knee at Therese's feet.

"You're the strongest, most beautiful woman I know," he told her. "Will you be my wife?" Therese laughed and said, "You're the most patient, most beautiful man I know. Of course, I will!"

—ɯ—

It did not surprise Luna when Therese went to work for a human rights organization in The City. They provided legal representation for women and children who had been displaced by militia groups. She often came home with sad stories, but usually, they ended in success. One day, as Luna was helping Felix get Mr. Muhangi into his bed, Therese stopped by the church. Through his four or five remaining teeth, Mr. Muhangi said, "Here comes our girl."

Therese kissed Mr. Muhangi on both cheeks and asked Felix, "How was school?"

Felix told her, "Hard. Fun. You know."

Brianna and her family still supported Felix. He attended university in The City, and he was studying to become a teacher like his father.

"How was work?" Luna asked. Therese sighed and said, "Hard. Fun. You know."

Luna did know. Her job was hard. The General's destruction was tremendous. There were thousands of displaced people who had lost their children, their parents, their jobs, and their land.

"A woman came in today with a great idea," Therese said. "She wants to make a well for her village. She has no clean drinking water, so she came in to discuss getting a permit to drill."

Mr. Muhangi spoke up. "I don't blame her. Clean water is important."

Therese sighed. "The land is in her late husband's name," she said. "The government won't grant her the permit." Luna asked Therese what she was going to do.

She stood up from Mr. Muhangi's nest. "Fight," she said.

She stretched her back and planted her hands on her hips. It was a pose Luna had seen so many times before.

—⁄⁄⁄⁄—

The years went by, and Therese continued to fight. Her skills as a lawyer merged well with her skills as an activist. Her successes outnumbered her failures, and she continued to make Luna proud. So did Felix. Once he finished graduate school in The City, he and Sylvia were married. He loved the church on the Long Road, and he took over running the grammar school there. By then they had their own priest. They had their own store, a bank, and a cell phone tower too. Manny and Sylvia also taught at the school in the church. With Mr. Muhangi's guidance, they had added classrooms to the building, and the lights, generated by the solar array on the church roof, never flickered.

With all the progress around them, some things never changed. Virgil never finished high school. His calling was on the boat. He added to the local economy by opening a fish market and butcher shop with Manny's father, Chui.

—⁄⁄⁄⁄—

On a bright, sunny morning in March, just days before Therese's twenty-fifth birthday, they buried Mr. Muhangi in the cemetery behind their church. The church had been his home until the day he died so it was fitting for his final resting place to be on its grounds. It was rare in Congo that someone lived to such an advanced age. Luna looked to the crowd assembled. None were his blood relatives, and yet all were his family. And they all mourned him. He had never remarried; most of the women his age were dead. But it had been enough for him in the end, to be surrounded by a community of people who loved him.

Herve held Luna's hand, as she wept into his shoulder. Virgil said, "Mr. Muhangi was the only person who ever understood me."

Felix and Sylvia filled Mr. Muhangi's boat with flowers and pushed it off the pier into the lake. For the first time in generations, the holes in the hull were too many, and the vessel slowly sank to the bottom. There was a collective gasp from the crowd, but really, it seemed a fitting end for the old boat. There would never be another captain like Mr. Muhangi.

That evening, after the mourners had all gone home, Therese and Luna walked hand-in-hand to the repair shop. Herve and Robert were helping Virgil finish his new fishing boat. Luna could hear the sounds of saws and sanders from across the highway. Halogen lights blazed from inside the windows. Therese turned to Luna and said, "Without Mr. Muhangi, we would have had no village." It was true. Mr. Muhangi had defended the church on the Long Road until one by one, they all found their way home.

EPILOGUE

~~~~~~~~~

Luna watches Therese and Felix's children play together like siblings. One minute, they are the best of friends, and the next, they are bitter enemies. They have learned the treasure hunt game that their parents taught them. Luna watches them hide from each other in the cassava and try to translate the English words they have learned. The baby of Therese's family, JP, squints at the handwriting on a scrap of paper his cousin has left him. *Toward the lake*, it reads. JP cannot remember the word "toward" in English, and asks his older sister, Mtume, what it means. She scolds him and tells him that if he had been paying attention to his lessons, he would know. He is only seven and begins to cry in frustration. Luna goes to him and dries his eyes on her dress.

"It's not fair!" he wails. Luna listens with attentiveness. His feelings are normal for a seven-year-old, but his frustration will pass. She tries not to diminish his feelings, but Luna realizes they are small compared to those of the adults around him, who have endured so much.

This child and his cousins are lucky. They will have the life that their parents did not. Therese goes to work every day and fights for the land rights of her people. She dedicates herself to making her country a peaceful place, and to finding educational opportunities for Congo's women and girls. She knows that if girls in DRC remain uneducated, they will continue to suffer. They will be violated, used, and treated as an expendable resource by cruel men like The General.

If Luna could wipe away even one small measure of her children's suffering, she would—and yet that terrible day in the cassava field rewrote their entire lives. Now Therese is helping to rewrite the lives of all girls in Congo, helping them to survive, succeed, and lead. Luna thinks about what they all lost on the day that the village burned—their loved ones, their health, their freedom, their land—and what they have managed to salvage. It is a bittersweet moment when Luna watches JP return to the game and, in front of his cousins, push his big sister into the mud. Mtume falls on her hands and knees with a cry of protest. Luna sends her a mind-message: Rise, rise, rise.

ACKNOWLEDGMENTS

This all started with Adam and Eve. I am indebted to the wise and warm Adam Hochschild, the author of *King Leopold's Ghost*, who illuminated the flickering light bulb over my head. Eve Ensler, Christine Schuler-Deschryver, and V-Day taught me about the current struggles of women in Congo. *City of Joy* is a true beacon in the darkness, and I am proud to be part of it. The 11th Hour Project provided transportation and wonderful learning opportunities. Anneke, Ida, and the Africa division of Human Rights Watch hosted me in DRC and kept me focused on the human tragedy and resilience in Congo. Denis Mukwege of Panzi Hospital, Emmanuel DeMerode of Virunga National Park, and the staff at Heal Africa, and the grassroots partners of the Fund for Global Human Rights are some of the special friends in the Democratic Republic of Congo who contributed to my education. Thank you to the girls and women of Congo, who taught me how strong females can be. Special thanks go to Herve, who got me off the mountain in the dark.

Closer to home, I could not have made this book happen without the generosity and love of my writing partners, Dorothy O'Donnell and Shannon Takaoka. Fellow writer and BFF, Jennifer Shiman, commiserated with me on the subjectivity of art. Mary Beth McClure, Maria Dudley, and Beth Touchette gave me encouragement, and Write On Mamas, especially Jessica O'Dwyer, Lorrie

Goldin, Janine Kovac, Meika Rouda, and Laurel Hilton, cheered from the sidelines. Barbara Ascher and Rosemarie Robotham, early champions of my manuscript, provided keen editorial eyes and wordsmithing advice. Thank you, Ally Sheedy, for excellent early feedback.

My cousin Amy Lehman and the Lake Tanganyika Floating Health Clinic gave me early inspiration. My cousin Susie Medak shared important contacts. Ira Hirschfield boldly suggested I go back to Congo after my first trip. Ragdale Residency for the Arts gave me shelter from my personal storm in the summer of 2018. Thank you, Martin and Judith Shepard and Nick Collins of The Permanent Press, for trusting me to write a very serious book during a very serious pandemic. I am so fortunate that you needed something to take your mind off sheltering in place!

I am grateful to copy editor Barbara Anderson for her eagle eyes. Thank you, Lon Kirschner, for creating a powerful and compelling cover. A special shout-out goes to my friend Kathleen Harrison, who always makes me look good.

Thanks to my Dadder, Dave Weinberg, and to my Brudder, Brian Weinberg, for worrying about me when I traveled to Congo. With unwavering support, you propped me up when I faltered and cheered me on to the finish line.

My sons, Ethan and Alex, have lived with this novel for the majority of their lives. They forgave me when I went to the DRC, writing retreats, and residencies, and they always hugged me when I got back. During the writing of this book, they each struggled and overcame challenges of their own, and they provided excellent role models in resilience for me.

The biggest thanks go to my husband, Kirk, who: kept home fires burning, helped expedite visas, assisted with computer/ formatting/luddite problems, explained statistical probability of success after rejection, read shitty drafts, came to speaking events, bragged about me, let me bitch about agents, toasted my accomplishments, smoothed my ruffled feathers, and loved me through it all. I am so lucky.

HOW CAN YOU HELP?

Donate to Human Rights Watch at www.hrw.org. Check out their Africa department!

For historical reference, read Adam Hochschild's *King Leopold's Ghost*: A Story of Greed, Terror, and Heroism in Colonial Africa

To learn about women's ability to heal, watch V-Day's *City of Joy* movie and donate to V-Day at www.vday.org.

Read about what the Lake Tanganyika Floating Health Clinic is doing in Congo at www.floatingclinic.org.

Read about the Virunga Rangers' Fund at www.virunga.org, and watch the *Virunga* film.

Donate to the Fund for Global Human Rights, especially to their grassroots partners in the Democratic Republic of the Congo at www.globalhumanrights.org.